The Phoebe Anderson Series

Finding
Phoebe

To my husband, Jeff:

Thank you for always believing in me, especially when I find it so hard to believe in myself.

To my parents, David and Lydia:

Thank you for raising me in a Jesus centered home and helping to make my dreams come true.

The Phoebe Anderson Series

Finding Phoebe

Chalaine Cuthbert Komadoski

Published by: ADVANTAGE BOOKS™
Orlando, FL.
www.advbookstore.com

All bible verses are taken from She Reads Truth Bible version of the bible. Copyright 2017 by Holman Bible Publishers.

Library of Congress Catalog Number: 2024939347	
Name:	Komadoski, Chalaine Cuthbert Author
Title:	Finding Phoebe
	Chalaine Cuthbert Komadoski
	Advantage Books, 2024
Identifiers:	ISBN Paperback: 9781597557955
	ISBN eBook: 9781597558068
	ISBN Hardcover: 9781597558174
Subjects:	RELIGION: Christian – Fiction

First Printing: October 2024
24 25 26 27 28 29 30   10 9 8 7 6 5 4 3 2 1

Chapter One

"Come on out, Phoebe. You promised you would show us ALL the dresses, if I took you to get mocha chocolate chip ice cream before we went home. I fully intend to keep my promise, if you do." Phoebe's oldest sister, Mary, yelled through the change room door, while knocking endlessly.

"Fine, fine, but you better be getting me two large scoops of ice cream for coming out in this horrible frock," Phoebe mumbled as she turned to look at herself in the mirror. It was the fifth dressed she tried on at Stacey's Boutique. It was a bubble gum pink dress with a large tulle bottom. The straps on it were ruffled tulle to match. Phoebe stepped out of the change room and glared at the women in front of her. "Alright, who picked this one out. Please, tell me it's a joke." Her three sisters and mom stared at her silently and then finally broke out into a fit of giggles.

"I picked it out!" said Tabitha breathlessly through her laughs. "I really thought it looked nice on the hanger. Maybe, you just can't pull it off."

"Now, Tabby, that's not nice. That just simply is not the one for you, honey." Ruth Anderson, Phoebe's mom, stated with reassurance.

"Honestly, I am starting to feel like nothing in this store full of prom dresses is the one. I could just stick with my jeans and t-shirt, at least then I would be comfortable and feel like myself. Or, even better, I could just blow the whole thing off."

"You can't do that! Prom was one of the best experiences ever. If you don't go, you will totally regret it." Anna, Phoebe's second older sister graduated from high school the year before. She was head cheerleader, most popular girl in school and won Prom Queen.

"I think we have had very different high school experiences, Anna. I know I won't win Prom Queen; I won't even be in the running." Phoebe crossed her arms over her chest. She started to feel more and more ridiculous in the bubble gum monstrosity, not to mention the tulle straps were really starting to itch.

"That doesn't matter, Pheebs. I wasn't Prom Queen either and I loved Prom. We just need to find something that makes you feel more like you." Mary was always the most practical Anderson sister. Her wisdom always seemed well beyond her years. Phoebe pouted.

"That's because you had Andrew. I won't get asked to prom."

"You don't know that." Phoebe's mom gave her a sweet smile and ushered her back into the change room. "Now, why don't we try on the last two dresses you have in that room and go for ice cream, no matter what the outcome. I happen to know the green one in there would look stunning on you. I picked that one out." She gave Phoebe a little nudge and closed the door behind her. Phoebe could hear her mom whispering to her sisters. She was probably telling them to be overly excited about the next two dresses she was about to try on. She grabbed the forest green one her mom picked out for her. It was strapless with a small sweetheart neckline. Tugging it on, Phoebe couldn't believe it fit nicely. It hugged her tightly all the way down to her hips and the bottom flowed effortlessly to the floor. The fabric was a satin, but it wasn't too shiny. Phoebe looked in the mirror and was taken back by what she saw. He body looked really nice, and the green did play off her pale skin and dark brown hair attractively. It even made her blue eyes look turquoise. She opened the door and immediately heard the oohs and awes from her family.

"That looks absolutely beautiful on you." Mary clasps her hands together and nodded enthusiastically.

"Seriously stunning," agreed Anna.

"I liked the pink one, just not on you," Tabby said, looking bored.

"Tabby!" Phoebe's mom gave her a death glare. Tabitha tried to give a sweet smile and then slumped back into her chair. At this point, Phoebe couldn't blame her. They had been dress shopping all afternoon and the mall was going to close soon. Phoebe didn't understand why she had to go dress shopping already considering it was March and prom was months away. But

Anna promised she would want to get her options now so no one else would have the same dress or Phoebe wouldn't get stuck with a bad one.

"How do you feel in it?" Mary asked. All four women held their breath.

"I actually really like it. It feels different than all the other ones I've tried on. It is very simple, which I like, but still unique. It is definitely my number one so far.

"Yay! I knew this trip wouldn't be in vain. Okay, Pheebs, just try on the last one in there. I picked it out. I know your school hasn't voted for prom themes yet. If the theme does happen to be Black and White Formal, you can't wear that one." Anna pointed to the last black dress hanging in the dressing room.

"How do you know about the theme options?" Phoebe asked hustling back into the change room. She was falling more and more in love with the forest green dress her mom had found. She could not wait to get that mocha chocolate chip ice cream and go home. Her feet were killing her.

"Brittany told me. She asked me to go dress shopping with her, Laura, and Charlotte next week."

"Oh, you mean Brittany and her minions," Tabby mocked.

"Tabby that's not nice to say," Anna scolded. "They are really nice, and you don't even know them."

"That's what I heard Phoebe call them to her friends one day." Tabby pointed to the dressing room. Phoebe said nothing and rolled her eyes. Tabitha was only ten years old, but sometimes she seemed to be the seventeen-year-old in the family. As much as Phoebe loved her, she could be a real pain. Being so much younger she often got away with a lot of things the three of the older Anderson sisters would have been grounded for.

"Anyways, as last year's head cheerleader and Brittany is this year's, so sometimes I help her out with routine ideas and stuff. We still talk. We are cheer sisters." Anna was way too nice for her own good and sometimes oblivious. Phoebe decided to keep quiet about the popular girls for now. She was too tired to hear her mom explain that everyone needs love, and how God said the greatest commandment is to love. It was true; Phoebe knew it, but she didn't want to hear it right now.

"I am ready." Phoebe opened the door to the change room. The Anderson woman all were nodding with big smiles. The black dress had the same silhouette as the forest green, but the neckline was straight across and had sequence all over it. Usually, this would be way too flashy for Phoebe. She would have never tried it on by herself, but she really liked it. "What do you guys think?" she asked and twirled around.

"It looks so good on you!" Mary clapped her hands again. The rest of them nodded even more quickly.

"I like it too," Phoebe said staring at herself in the mirror. She felt grown up and sophisticated in it.

"You look amazing, sweetie." Phoebe's mom got up and gave her a quick hug.

"Thanks, mom." Phoebe smiled at her mom in return.

"I will tell Stacey to put these two on hold for you. That way we can make sure no one else will get them." Anna stood up quickly and made her way to the front counter, leaving her scent of sweet flowers behind.

"Now, Pheebs, why don't you get in your own clothes, and we will go get that ice cream," Phoebe's mom declared.

"Finally!" yelled Tabby. "But are you sure you don't want to get the pink one?"

"Yes!" all the Anderson women said at once laughing.

"I think you will be happy that you picked out those dresses so early, Pheebs. Once they announce the theme you should make your decision. Stacey said she would hold the dresses until then, but after that she has to make them available again," Anna stated factually as they walked towards the ice cream booth in the mall.

"Okay, I can do that." Phoebe didn't want to talk about it anymore. She knew that Anna loved the prom, but she just didn't feel as excited about it. All the Anderson sisters were so different. Just as different as their dress styles.

First was Mary. Mary was twenty-years-old and fitted the stereotype of the oldest sibling. She was logical, over achiever, respectful and very responsible. In high school, Mary was on the honour roll every year. She never really played on any sports teams, but was in several clubs. To everyone's surprise, the day after her sixteenth birthday she came home from school and said Andrew Parker was her boyfriend. She wasn't excited or nervous to say it; it was just a fact. She was dating Andrew Parker. No one in the Anderson family even knew boys were on Mary's radar. The Anderson sisters were not allowed to date until they turned sixteen, a well-known fact around town, thanks to the ever-popular Anna. When Mary said Andrew was her boyfriend, no one questioned her. Even Mr. Anderson had nothing bad or worrisome to say, because it was Mary. Andrew has been around ever since.

Anna was the next oldest and almost polar opposite from Mary. All the Anderson sisters had brown hair with blue eyes and paler skin, but none of them were as beautiful as Anna. Anna's hair was several shades lighter than the others, almost a dirty blond and wavy. Her blue eyes also were paler with a sparkle behind them, like she was always keeping a secret. As the boys at school said, "she was a knockout." Anna graduated from high school the year before. She was head cheerleader, prom queen, and the most beloved girl by her classmates. What Mary had in smarts and practicality, Anna had it in sweetness. She was nice to everyone and only saw their good qualities, never their bad. Currently, she was attending Fendry College, for hairdressing and cosmetology. When questioned about dating, she always said she liked to keep her options open. It seemed like everyone knew Anna wherever she went. She was Miss congeniality.

Tabitha was the youngest of the Anderson sisters. People would call her the "oops" of the family because she was almost a decade younger than Phoebe, but Ruth Anderson said she was a blessing. Tabitha, or Tabby as most people called her, was definitely the apodeme of the baby. She was spoiled and got away with way more than Phoebe or either older Anderson sister would, but her parents denied it. Tabby was also the clever trickster of the family. She could convince people of anything. Her big round blue eyes helped lure people in. Phoebe was convinced that Tabby would make an amazing Politian or mafia leader. Anytime she mentioned it, her mother would lecture her saying that God gives us each unique gifts that can all be used in ways to honour Him.

Phoebe Anderson was the third Anderson sister and currently in her senior year of high school. She felt like she was the plain jane of the family. She didn't excel at schoolwork, or social skills like her older sisters and didn't have the drive or strong will like Tabitha. Phoebe was still trying to find her "thing" as her dad would say. It's not that she wasn't good at school; she got mostly B's and she also had her friends, but she was not part of the popular crowd. She felt that she was okay looking. She liked her dark hair and dark blue eyes against her skin, and she shared her tiny button nose with Anna that they inherited from their mom. Phoebe felt she was just Phoebe. Just Phoebe.

"Mom, you promised me we could look at the dolls in the toy store before we went home. You said that if I came, we could go." Tabby was working her big blue round eyes against her very tired mother.

"I did promise that didn't I?" The Anderson matriarch stopped in front of the ice cream store. "Girls, get yourself what you want and grab Tabby and I a small shake each. That way we don't have to worry about it melting. Why don't we meet at the car in twenty minutes? We have to get home soon; it's almost dinnertime." Tabby had a huge smile plastered on her face as she tugged Ruth Anderson's arm in the direction of the toy store.

"Pheebs and Annie, why don't you go grab us a table, while I order our shakes?" Mary said as she moved into the line-up.

"I'll grab the straws!" Anna called as she flipped her dirty blonde wavy hair over her shoulder. When she came back to the small round table Phoebe found to sit at, she looked at Phoebe and asked, "How's it going with Mr. Xu? Has he lightened the load of work yet?" Mr. Xu was Phoebe's biology teacher and he thought everyone was just as passionate about the subject as he was - which meant an enormous about of reading every week.

"No, not yet. I hope the reading starts to die down soon though; I need the extra time every night to work on kinesiology. Memorizing the bones in my body has proven more difficult than I thought." Phoebe shrug.

"It will happen. As soon as you finish your study on marine mammals, he seems to be less interested in all other topics." Anna let out her contagious laugh. Another thing Phoebe was slightly envious of Anna for.

"Mammals! Mammals are wonderous creatures!" Phoebe started on her impression of Mr. Xu. She grabbed two straws that were laying on the table and put them under her top lips making it look like they were the tusks of a walrus. "Walruses are some of the most interesting marine mammals." Anna started to giggle even harder, which encouraged Phoebe to continue, "Did you know that if provoked a walrus could take down a polar bear?" Drool was now running down from the straws in Phoebe's mouth, but she kept going, "Did you also know that…"

"Hey, Anna!" a deep husky voice came from across the food court. Both Anna and Phoebe turned to see who it was coming from.

"Hey! How are you guys?" Anna called back. Three tall muscular built guys crossed the hall and headed towards their table. The owner of the voice was the second tallest of the three. He had caramel skin and short dark hair with the lightest green eyes Phoebe had ever seen.

"We're good. We came with Parker. He needed to pick up a birthday present for his mom." When he was explaining he kept stealing glances at Phoebe. Phoebe finally realized that she had the straws still tucked under her lip! She quickly pulled them out, but one of them left a string of spit hanging from her mouth to the straw. Phoebe could feel her face turn bright red. She couldn't look at any of the guys now standing around her table. Anna let out a giggle.

"That's really sweet; I hope that he is able to find something she will like. We were just prom dress shopping for my sister today. Finishing up a successful trip with some ice cream shakes," Anna disclosed. Phoebe peeked up at the three boys. The first was clearly interested in Anna and didn't break eye contact with her now that Phoebe had pulled the straws out of her lips. The second one was the shortest. He had longer blonde hair with bangs that swept over his forehead. His very square jaw was a good match for his full round lips. Phoebe couldn't tell what colour his eyes were because he was looking down at his phone, clearly not as into the conversation as his friend was. The third, was the tallest. He was wearing a Fendry Fire Hawk baseball cap. His short light brown hair came out from the sides, and he had scruff starting to show on his chin. He looked back over at Phoebe and smirked making her turn even a brighter shade of red. Their eyes connected and Phoebe could see they were a rich chocolatey brown colour. She quickly looked back down at the saliva soak straws.

"Girls' day! Well, don't let us stop you from enjoying those shakes. We will see you around!" Mr. green eyes said.

"For sure," Anna replied with a sweet smile. Phoebe could see why Mr. green eyes was smitten. The guys walked away, and Anna burst out laughing. Phoebe hit her forehead on the table.

"Who were they?" Mary asked as she approached the table carrying a tray filled with five shakes.

"Those guys are on the baseball team. Thomas, Leo, and Jasper. I have met them several times at sports events and fund-raisers, but don't see them much otherwise since we only cheer at the football games." Anna grabbed her shake from Mary and put one of the non-saliva straws in it to take a big sip.

"Well, Phoebe seemed to make a great impression on them." Mary and Anna both started to laugh uncontrollably. "What were you trying to be?" Mary asked trying to catch her breath.

"A walrus." Phoebe kept her eyes focused on the table. She couldn't even look up at her sisters. She totally just had the most embarrassing moment of her life. They were some of the cutest boys she had ever seen.

"Go grab some new straws and let's go meet mom and Tabby at the car," Mary said trying to stifle her laughter just a little bit. Phoebe did as Mary told her, still feeling the heat from her beet red cheeks. She knew that they would be that way for a long time with how ridiculous she felt.

Chapter Two

All the Anderson girls were in the car ready to hit the road. It would be a twenty-minute drive from the mall in Fendry to their home in Hillwood. Hillwood was just a tiny community. It contained all the necessities, nothing outside of that. Fendry was the closest city to Phoebe's hometown. It was where the college was - home of the Fire Hawks, the mall, movie theatres, etc.

"Mary, could you, please, call your father and ask him to start dinner. If he waits until I get home, we won't be able to eat until seven. Is Andrew coming? Make sure you tell you father, so we know how many steaks to put on the BBQ." Mrs. Anderson pulled onto the highway using her one hand to instruct Mary.

"Sure mom, and yes, Andrews's coming again. His mom has to work a long shift at the hospital tonight." Mary pulled out her phone to call her dad and relay her mom's instructions. Andrew was often over at the Andersons' for dinner. His mother was a well-respected E.R. doctor and often worked. You could tell how much Andrew admired and respected his mother for the work she did for the community. Phoebe always wondered though if he was a bit resentful because she was never home. He never said he was. Phoebe had grown accustomed to having Andrew around. Mary and Andrew had been together well over four years now. Everyone knew they were meant to be, but Mary refused to even talk about the idea of marriage until she completed her education. She was going to school to become a veterinarian at Fendry College, and Andrew wanted to be an osteopath. They were both only twenty and twenty-one and had at least three more years of schooling left to do.

Phoebe put her head on the window in the backseat and felt the cold glass cool down her inflamed embarrassed cheeks. Luckily, neither Mary nor Anna had said anything to mom yet about her moment with the baseball boys.

Usually, the girls told her mom everything. Phoebe didn't mind, she just didn't want Tabby to find out because then the whole world would find out. Tabby was in the middle of the backseat talking to Anna about all the ways she could style her new doll's hair. Phoebe smiled and wondered how she got away with getting one this time. She clearly remembered her mom telling Tabby they were just going to look. *The political mastermind manipulator strikes again,* Phoebe thought.

Luckily, the drive went by quickly and they pulled in the driveway. Andrew's car was already there.

"I am going to go call Jenn; I promised her I would let her know how prom dress shopping went today," Phoebe said, hustling to the front door.

"Ok, sweetie, but only ten minutes, hopefully, if your dad didn't forget anything we will be eating soon." Phoebe nodded her head, grabbed the portable phone off the table by the stairs and ran up, taking two steps at a time. She went into her small bedroom. Phoebe used to have to share a bedroom with Tabby, but when Tabby started snoring during allergy season and kept getting pillows in the head waking her up, their parents decided they should be separated. Anna and Mary share what was the master bedroom, while their parents built a huge master suit in the basement of the house. Tabby had the next largest room and that left Phoebe with the smallest. It was just big enough for her single bed, dresser, desk, and tiny bookshelf. Phoebe loved it, though. There was a window seat, and she could look out onto the front yard.

"Hello?" Jenn's voice rang out on the other side of the line.

"Hey, Jenn," Phoebe stretched out on her twin bed ready to dish on her afternoon.

"Pheebs! Did you find one? What does it look like?" Jennifer Carter was one of Phoebe's best friends. They had been best friends since elementary school. Jenn had two passions in life, sports, and fashion.

"I found two options. Anna made a good point in saying that I should wait until the senior class votes for a theme."

"You're so lucky that you had Anna to go with you. She has great taste and somehow, she is able to pick out something that is approved by parental figures. My dad keeps telling me that I have to make sure I am displaying good choices with my fashion. Something that God would be happy with me wearing." Jenn sighed on the phone.

"I am sure she would love to go with you, if you asked her. Apparently, she is going with Brittany and her crowd to give advice." Phoebe tried not to sound too betrayed.

"Maybe, I will ask her. I mean, I would take you, but I know you hate it, and I really don't want to go with just my dad. I was also thinking I could possibly use the dress I am making for my school project. I would have to get permission to change the assignment a bit, but I don't think it would be too big of a problem. I would love to be able to say I wore my own design to prom." Jenn was an only child and raised by her father. Her mother left when she was two years old. Jenn actually thinks her dad might have kicked her out because she was addicted to drugs. Either way, Jenn never complained. Her father was her hero. "So, tell me about your two options."

"The first one is a beautiful satin forest green; my mom actually picked it out. It is strapless and has a small sweetheart neckline. It hugs me at my hips and then goes straight to the bottom." Phoebe was using her free hand to explain what she meant even though she knew Jenn couldn't see her.

"Oh, yes, an A-line dress would definitely look great on your body type. What's the second one?"

"It's black strapless with a straight neckline and the same shape as the green one." An A-line or whatever Jenn had called it. "But get this! It is covered in black sequence!"

"No!" Jenn gasped in disbelief. "I can't believe you even put that on let alone like it! Look at you, expanding your horizons."

"I know," Phoebe giggled. She usually preferred her ripped jeans and comfy t-shirts. Plain Phoebe. "So, I would wear the black if prom is voted to be the black and white theme or the green one if not." Phoebe was actually surprising herself with how excited she sounded and felt.

"Did you get them set aside? Did you take pictures?" Jenn questioned her best friend.

"Yes, Anna put them aside and no I totally didn't think to get pictures; it was the last store we went to. I didn't think I was going to find anything, but then I did. Thank goodness because I don't think I could handle another afternoon full of trying on dresses."

"Phoebe! Dinnertime!" Phoebe's mom yelled up the stairs.

"Sorry, Jenn, I have to go."

"No problem. Hey, could you maybe mention it to Anna about me needing someone to go shopping with? Or maybe if she would be willing to look at some of my sketches? I am really curious about what she would think of them. See if they could be prom material?" Phoebe could hear the hesitance in Jenn's voice. She thought it must be hard to be the only girl in the family. Phoebe was one of five, she always had someone to ask girly advice.

"Sure, I know she will say yes. I'll talk to you later!"

"Bye!" Phoebe heard Jenn hang up the phone and she bounded down the stairs to the dinner table. Everyone was sitting there waiting for her to join.

"Hey, Pheebs," Andrews said nodding his head at her, while passing around a bowl of mashed potatoes.

"Hey." Phoebe took her usual spot at the table and helped herself to the bowl of salted buttery corn on the cob. "This looks amazing, dad, thanks for cooking dinner."

"See, I can cook!" Phoebe dad said self-defensively. She must have missed something while she was on the phone with Jenn.

"I never said you couldn't, sweetie," her mom replied passing out the steaks. Phoebe definitely missed something.

"So, I heard dress shopping went well." John Anderson was not very into fashion, but he loved all of his girls the most in the world. Keeping in touch with them was very important to him.

"Yes, I found some that I really liked. Thanks again for all the help everyone." Phoebe smiled.

"You'll look beautiful in whatever one you pick." Mrs. Anderson replied.

"I still think you should pick the pink one," Tabby giggled, helping herself to one of the biggest steaks on the plate. Phoebe rolled her eyes at her little sister.

"What are everyone's plans for tomorrow?" Mr. Anderson asked.

"Tomorrow, Andrew and I are going to volunteer at the pet shelter in Fendry. They are doing a big push to find all of the pets new homes." Mary sounded very excited. She truly did love animals. Andrew just nodded his head while he chopped into his steak.

"Tabby promised that I could practice some up-dos on her tomorrow," Anna said.

"Only if you give me a manicure that I want. No more French tips. That's just so boring. I want something with life, with pizazz." Tabby flung her hand up into the air dramatically.

"Yes, I promise, but just so you know French tips are very sophisticated." Tabby made a face at Anna showing that she really didn't care. "Then it is also HSCC tomorrow night." Anna continued on ignoring Tabby's faces. HSCC was the High school, College, and Career group for their church. Usually, the two groups were separated and alternated Saturday nights. But getting closer to the end of the school year the church combined the two groups every once and a while. That way all the teens and young adults could get to know one another, especially those transitioning into college, like Phoebe. The leaders thought it was a good way to show support and keep everyone united.

"You can only go if you finish all your homework before; that goes for all of you." Phoebe's dad pointed his fork at them. "Are you working tomorrow, Phoebe?"

"Yes, I said I would come in for the early morning shift. I only have to work until noon. I don't think I'll make HSCC, though. I have so much reading to do." Phoebe shrugged. She hated missing out on HSCC, but she knew she would hate falling behind even more in biology than she already was.

"Ah, yes, have to read up on how to better impersonate a walrus, right?" Phoebe's dad winked at her. Everyone around the table started laughing. Phoebe could feel the heat returning back to her cheeks. Great, everyone knew. All she could do now was join in with the laughing at her most embarrassing moment ever.

Chapter Three

Phoebe smacked her alarm clock to turn it off. How could it already be 5:00am? She regretted immediately staying up and watching Extreme Days for the millionth time with Mary and Andrew. They all loved that movie and could quote it word for word. It seemed like a good idea to watch it last night, but now having only five hours of sleep she knew it was definitely a mistake. Phoebe shuffled out of bed and grabbed some jeans and a t-shirt. Luckily, she was just starting the bread this morning, so she didn't need to actually work the counter at Barker's Bakery. Phoebe started working at the bakery when she turned sixteen. Her dad said that if any of the girls wanted to drive the car they had to pay for their portion of the insurance. The Bakery was a ten-minute bike ride from the house and had flexible hours for Phoebe to work. Plus, she just loved the smell and atmosphere of the place. It was perfect for her. She started with just two days a week after school for a few hours, but now that she was getting ready to go to college, hopefully, she began working Saturday mornings as well. She knew her dad would pay for tuition, but not books. It really was a fair trade. Even though it was so hard to get up early on the one day she could sleep in, she loved being there in the quiet before all the customers came. Preparing the dough for the different breads, getting the coffee brewing, and setting out all the Saturday's specials was Phoebe's favourite. The aroma alone was heavenly. Phoebe hustled herself to the bathroom and put her long brown hair up into a ponytail. She quickly did her basic makeup consisting of light foundation, mascara, and some lip gloss. Shaking off the tired feeling, she went down the stairs to the garage. Anna and Tabby had requested to use their shared car this morning so that they could run to the drugstore and pick up some needed supplies for Anna's hair creations. Phoebe didn't mind she knew that riding her bike in the brisk air would really help wake she up. She was just thankful that there wasn't any more snow on the ground. Hopefully spring would be right around the corner.

Phoebe had made it just to work with 5 minutes to spare, 5:25. She used her key to unlock the door and Mrs. Barker was already inside turning on the lights in the front glass counter.

"Good morning, dear!" Mrs. Barker exclaimed. Phoebe loved Mrs. Barker. She reminded her of Mrs. Potts from Beauty and the Beast. She was a rounder woman with white hair and a British accent.

"Good morning, Mrs. Barker. How are you?" Phoebe walked behind the counter and into the backroom to put her bag and coat away.

"Oh, just lovely!" Mrs. Baker was always "just lovely". "Your cheeks are so red from the wind. I can't believe you rode your bike here in this cold weather." Mrs. Barker shook her head and laughed.

"I don't mind. It helped wake me up. Anna needed the car this morning anyways." Phoebe smiled.

"Well why don't you start the coffee and hot chocolate makers and fill the hot water dispenser. Then you can make yourself something warm to drink before we get started. Today is cinnamon loaf day!" Mrs. Barker waved her hand at the coffee station and hurried out back to get the ingredients ready. Phoebe loved making the cinnamon loaves. She smelt like Christmas for the rest of the day. Sometimes the smell even lingered in her hair a few days after, if she didn't wash it. Mrs. Barker must have turned on the music over the store's speakers. Worship music quietly filled the room. That was another reason why Phoebe loved working for Mrs. Barker; she was a Christian woman and was not afraid to show it. Sometimes they would get complaints about the music. One customer said he felt they were pushing their religion on him, but Mrs. Barker said he was more than welcome to stay, but if he was uncomfortable, he could leave as well. She didn't change the music. She loved how Mrs. Barker stood firm in her faith; Phoebe wanted to be able to do the same thing. Growing up going to secular schools sometimes made it difficult for her. A lot of her classmates would tease her about not being able to listen to certain music or attend R rated movies. She had to admit sometimes it made her feel awkward and lonely. She wanted to be able to be confident and not be afraid to say what she believes, even when she was still trying to figure that all out for herself. She believed in God; she asked him to come into her life when she was little. She was even baptized in grade eight proclaiming her faith to others, but sometimes she felt so disconnected from God. Was He listening to her? Did He care about her? Her parents taught her stories from the bible and would quote bible verses to her and her sisters. But sometimes their way of saying things made it feel like following God was a bunch of rules, not a real relationship that she was longing for. They always said to just be who God made her to be, like it was so simple. Who was that, though? Phoebe didn't know yet. She felt like she was searching for herself and God at the same time. It was overwhelming.

Phoebe went over and started all the hot beverages and grabbed two cups. One for her and one for Mrs. Barker. She was so thankful for her job. She knew how lucky she was to have another adult figure in her life that was a believer, especially her boss.

The bakery opened its doors at nine on Saturdays and was open until two. The prep person only had to stay until twelve, though. Phoebe loved being the prep person. Not that she didn't enjoy working the counter and interacting with the customers, but she much rather be making the delicious treats and snacking on some - just to make sure that they turned out okay. It worked out well, no one else wanted to wake up that early on Saturdays anyway.

Phoebe wiped off her hands on her apron glancing around the room at everything she had accomplished this morning. Satisfied with it all, she cleaned up the kitchen and herself ready to head home.

"Bye, Mrs. Barker, I will see you on Tuesday!" Phoebe shouted from the backroom into Mrs. Barker's office.

"Okay, sweetie, thanks for all your help, as always." Mrs. Baker step outside her office door. "You've got any plans this weekend?"

"Yeah, my homework. I feel like I am a bit behind in my readings. I really need to keep up my grades, if I want to get that scholarship to Fendry. Any bit helps." Phoebe knew her dad would pay for tuition, but putting four girls through college was not going to be a financially easy task.

"Well, make sure you have some fun this weekend. A beautiful girl like you can't be cooped up all the time reading; you'll turn into a book yourself!" Mrs. Barker laughed at her own joke. "Are you at least going to HSCC tonight? It is a great time for you to make some friends before heading off to college. Friendly faces will definitely be nice to have that first week, believe me. I may be old, but I remember." Mrs. Barker had a smirk on her face. It looked like she was reminiscing about her college times. Phoebe wanted to know what she was thinking, but didn't feel right to pry.

"I can't this time, but I will go to the next one. I promise."

"Alrighty, see you Tuesday, sweetie." Mrs. Baker walked back into her office and Phoebe was off back on her bike for the ride home.

When Phoebe got home, she was chilled to the bone from the brisk air on the ride back. She decided to make soup for lunch and then jump in the shower to warm the rest of her body before hitting the books for the rest of the day, which passed by quickly. Before she knew it, her mom had called her down for dinner, scalloped potatoes and ham, one of her favourites.

"How is your homework going, hon?" Mom asked her.

"Okay, I finished all my reading; I just have to finish up one more assignment." Phoebe was so glad that she has accomplished so much in a day.

"You know, you have been working really hard today. You could go to HSCC tonight, as long as you finish your work tomorrow." Dad gave her an approving nod. Phoebe loved it when she could see how proud her father was of her work ethic. He didn't often say it, but she could see it in his eyes.

"No, I think I will stay home today. If I finish it tonight, then tomorrow I will have the whole day off." Phoebe's dad nodded again making her feel like she made the right decision.

"Well, Mary, Anna, and Tabby, you can help your mother do the dishes and Phoebe go get started on your last assignment. Tomorrow, since you are all done your homework, I was thinking I could take you all out for lunch after church."

"Sounds lovely," Mrs. Anderson said. The Andersons usually only went out to eat on special occasions. Mr. Anderson thought it was too expensive to feed all six of them when they could just relax and have a cheaper meal at home. Everyone started to move to do their allocated job. Even Tabby didn't complain about having to help do the dishes. She loved going out to lunch. She probably knew that if she complained it would get taken away or she would be at least threatened with it. Still, Phoebe was still a little surprised that her baby sister didn't even grumble.

"Hey, Dad, since the other girls are busy tonight could I watch a movie on TV? It is the weekend and all?" Tabby used her sweetest voice.

And there it is… Phoebe thought. She knew her cunning sister must have something up her sleeve to be so agreeing. She smiled and shook her head as she climbed up the stairs determined to have a homework-free Sunday.

Later, Phoebe heard the sounds of laughter filtering through up the stairs and down the hallway and into her bedroom. Her sisters must be home from HSCC at church. She peered at her clock through tired eyes. Yes, it was just after ten. Phoebe had finished her homework about fifteen minutes earlier and was laying on her bed. Her brain too tired to control her limbs to move. She was, however, ecstatic that she was going to have a work-free Sunday. That hadn't happened in quite a while. The laughter continued on downstairs, and she wanted to go see what was so funny. Giving up, she promised herself a cup of tea, headed down the hall trying to be quiet so she wouldn't wake up Tabby. Although, if something was going to wake her up it would be the laughing.

"What's so funny?" she asked as she went to turn on the kettle and sat down at the table with Mary and Anna.

"We played the funniest game tonight at HSCC. I am really sad you missed it; but I am proud of the decision you made to stay home." Phoebe smiled back at the ever-practical Mary. Of course, she was proud of Phoebe's very logical decision.

"I think you should have taken dad up on his offer and came." Anna said, still red faced and giggling. "There were some people there asking about you and why you didn't come tonight."

"What are you talking about?" Phoebe asked glancing back and forth between Mary and Anna. Mary smirked and got up and grabbed some cups to make Sleepy Time Tea, their classic nighttime girl talk drink.

"Do you remember those guys from the mall yesterday? The baseball players?" Phoebe's heart started to beat a little faster. "Those ones that caught you acting like a walrus?" Mary almost dropped a cup trying not to laugh.

"Yes, I remember them, why?" Phoebe asked slowly and carefully, wanting to know the answer to the question.

"Well, apparently, Thomas and Jasper were in town today helping out Thomas' aunt; I think you know her from church, Alison Hernandez. She mentioned to them that HSCC was on tonight at the church and they wanted to check it out." Anna was now sipping her tea waiting to see Phoebe's reaction. Phoebe was trying to keep a straight face, for some reason she had massive butterflies in her stomach. "Anyways, we were all talking at the beginning, and they asked me where my "straws sister" was tonight. I told them you were being lame and doing homework. Oh, and that you were my walrus sister!"

"WHAT! Anna, why did you do that?" Phoebe didn't know if she was madder at her sister for saying that to some of the cutest boys she had ever seen, or to be more excited because they had actually asked about her?

"Don't worry, Pheebs; they laughed. They were wondering what you were trying to do though." Mary gave her a sympathetic look.

"Did you say anything else about me?" Phoebe tried not to sound to obvious and hopeful for their attention.

"No, we started right after that. Then they seemed to be occupied by Brittany, Laura, and Charlotte." Anna shrugged and sipped her tea again. Phoebe tried not to appear to be disappointed. She wondered if Anna was upset that they didn't pay more attention to her. Phoebe was upset and she wasn't even there. Anna didn't appear to be. She liked to explore her relationship options. She liked to be free as a bird. Phoebe wished that she could feel that way, but then again, she knew she wasn't as adored as Anna by every guy in town. This was another area where Anna and Phoebe were different. Phoebe had never had a boyfriend, had never been asked out on a proper date and had never kissed anyone before. Sure, she had elementary school crushes and had hung out in groups before with a boy she had liked but nothing had ever develop from there. At first, she thought it was because everyone knew the Anderson girls couldn't date until they turned sixteen, but in the past two years she had never been asked out. Her sisters brough it up with her once. Anna had said not to worry about it; when the right guy comes it will happen. Mary had told her that she needed to be more confident in herself. That she was shy and that it made boys feel like she was unapproachable. Tabby had overheard the conversation and told Phoebe maybe she was just unlikeable. Phoebe was terrified that Tabby was right but tried to convince herself it was a combination of Mary and Anna's observations. This year she had really been working on becoming more confident in herself and really focusing on figuring out who she was.

"Well, I don't know about you two, but I need to go to bed. I didn't realize how tired I was." Anna picked up her teacup and put it in the sink. Mary followed. Before they started walking up the stairs, Mary turned around and looked at Phoebe.

"I did hear one of them telling Andrew that they would be coming to church tomorrow with Mrs. Hernandez. So maybe you want to go to bed and get some sleep too." She winked and followed Anna to their shared bedroom. Phoebe's heart rate started to pick up. Why was she getting so nervous about seeing Thomas and Jasper again? She didn't even know which face belonged to which name. Maybe it was just the fact that someone actually remembered who she was. Nevertheless, she ran upstairs to her bedroom to try and get some sleep, even though it would be so hard. She laid down in her bed and thanking God for all her blessings and also asking that she wouldn't look like a zombie tomorrow morning.

Chapter Four

Phoebe woke up extra early on Sunday so that she could beat the rest of her sisters to the one bathroom they shared. Her parents, thankfully, when they built their bedroom in the basement also created a bathroom just for themselves. They deserved their little oasis, but sometimes a small bathroom for four girls was unbearable. When she finished her shower, she took the blow-dryer and her makeup bag into her room. She knew that the others would be wanting in soon and her chances of grabbing anything she needed would be slim. She had dried her long hair straight and found a cute blue clip and pinned one side back. She wore her makeup light, since her parents would not allow their daughters to wear a bunch of it but added a few extra coats of mascara. She felt like her eyes were bigger and brighter. She found her black high waisted cigarette paints and pulled them on. She slipped on her white top with shear sleeves that had cute little blue flowers on it that match her hair clip. Phoebe felt really pretty and put together. She just hoped that her sisters wouldn't tease her about trying to look really nice today, now that she knew Thomas and Jasper might be at church. Soon Phoebe's mom called from downstairs that it was time to go. The chaos ensued. Phoebe could hear Anna yelling at Tabby to hurry up and get out of the bathroom. Mary was yelling at Anna, asking her what she did with her pink sweater she borrowed last week. Phoebe walked down the stairs holding her black high heels in her hands. Normally she didn't like wearing heels because she was afraid to fall on her face and that it would add too much height to her 5'7" frame. However, they looked great with her pants.

"Wow, Phoebe, you look stunning today," Mrs. Anderson said as she buttoned up her coat.

"Thanks, Mom." Phoebe felt herself blush and made a mental note that she needed to work on controlling the colour of her cheeks.

"Anna you are not allowed to wear anymore of my clothes until you replace that pink sweater! It was my favourite. I feel like sometimes you are just so careless!" Mary was shaking her head and stomping down the stairs with Anna trailing behind her.

"I'm ready!" Tabby called from the top of the stairs. She had a huge smile on her face, and everyone could see the bright red lipstick she was wearing.

"Tabby, where in the world did you get that lipstick from?" Mrs. Anderson asked, shocked.

"I found it in the makeup drawer in the bathroom. I like it." Tabby took big confident steps down the stairs. Phoebe knew that her mother was not impressed. She would never have let the three older girls wear lipstick at Tabby's age. She was only ten.

"Tabby, that's my game day lipstick for cheer! You better have not mushed it all over the lid like you do to every other lip-gloss I have!" Anna yelled at her sister. Phoebe felt the tension rising. Today was going to be one of those days where the Anderson sisters were at each other's throats. It didn't happen often, which was actually surprising for all the estrogen in the house, but when it did watch out. Phoebe slowly crept out the door and met her father in their family van. She could hear the arguing all the way outside.

"What is going on in there Pheebs?" Mr. Anderson asked as he looked at Phoebe in the review mirror when she climbed into one of the middle seats. Phoebe sometimes wondered how her dad felt about having to live with five women. It must be really hard. No wonder he loved it so much when Andrew came over. It was another male in the house. He also was an avid fisherman and no matter what was happening with his landscaping business he made sure that he always could make the men's fishing retreat at church.

"Tabby found Anna's bright red lipstick for cheer and is wearing it. Anna doesn't want her to wreck it, mom doesn't want Tabby to wear it. Anna lost Mary's favourite sweater; she wants a new one." Phoebe shrugged. She was just glad no arrows were pointed at her yet. Mr. Anderson rolled his eyes, which made Phoebe laugh.

"Well, if we don't get going, we are going to be really late, and I am supposed to be an usher today." Mr. Anderson honked the horn and the rest of the Anderson women spilled out of the house. They all looked frustrated with each other; except Tabby who was still wearing the red lipstick and sashaying her way to the van.

"Everyone get in, please. I am supposed to usher today." Mr. Anderson called out the window.

"Sorry, honey." Phoebe's mom gracefully pulled herself into the front seat of the van. It was a very silent ride to church, which wasn't too far from where the Anderson's lived. When Mr. Anderson pulled into the parking lot instead of unlocking the doors he made sure they were locked. He turned around to face his four daughters.

"Now, today is the Lord's Day and I will not have my family going into His house with grumpy ungrateful faces and hearts. You girls have so much to be thankful for, especially each other. So, I am going to sort this outright now and we are not going to talk about it again. Does everyone understand?" They all nodded. When dad got involved, you did as he said. "Anna you will either find the sweater that your sister let you borrow by Wednesday, or you will buy her a new one and give it to her on Friday. If you do not, you will give her the amount it cost, or you will be restricted from friend outings for two weeks. You need to be more responsible with other people's items." Mary looked satisfied and a bit smug about that ruling until Mr. Anderson looked over to her. "Mary, you need to treat people with respect and better understanding. You are the oldest and I expect you to be a good example." Mary just nodded at her father trying to keep her head held high. Even thought she was almost twenty-one, Phoebe knew that their father's words always had affected Mary to her core. "Tabby, you are far too young to be wearing any kind of makeup right now, especially something so flashy. Now, I am assuming your mother let you wear it because we didn't have time to scrub it off. However, consider this your lucky day that you get to wear it. You, young lady, are not allowed to wear makeup yet and you know that. Please, do not disappoint me by breaking those rules."

"Yes, Daddy," Tabby said giving her best sweet cutesy face, but today their dad was having none of it.

"Now, let's go." With that he unlocked the doors which signaled the conversation was over and no one would bring it up again. They filed inside. Tabby ran down the hallway to her Sunday school class. Phoebe guessed it was for fear that her parents would change their mind and make her go to the bathroom to scrub off the bright red lipstick. Phoebe knew if she had pulled that stunt at Tabby's age, she would have been forced to wash it off. No sense fighting or bringing it up. She had gotten out of the van without a lecture, and she wanted to keep it that way. Her dad also ran off to the office to get ready to usher and her mom must have disappeared down the hall to the kitchen to see if anything needed to be done. Their church used to be one of those small white churches where you walked in the door and was directly in the auditorium already. It had been renovated many years ago, but from the front still looked like a tiny church. The addition had been put on the back. There was a small front area right when you walked in that lead to the doors to the new auditorium where the service was held. There were also hallways to the left and right that made a large circle around the old church. You could go either way and make it back to the same spot you started. There were mainly classrooms to the right and to the left were church staff offices, all the way at the back was the kitchen and church gym. Phoebe loved their church. It's cute white façade, wooden doors and tall steeple made her feel like she was in the olden days. She always imagined getting married at this church and having all her guest stand out front for a group picture.

"I am going to go find Andrew. His mom is here today so we are sitting with her," Mary said and stalked away. It was obvious to Phoebe that she was still feeling the weight of their father's words and frustration with Anna.

"Hey, Anna!" Anna and Phoebe both turned their heads at the sound of deep friendly voice. Two stunning handsome males walked towards them. It was Thomas and Jasper.

"Hi, Thomas," Anna waved to one of them. Phoebe finally knew which one was which from that little wave. Thomas was wearing navy blue paints with a crisp white long sleeve shirt that was unbuttoned at the top. His dark features definitely played up by the white of the shirt. Next to him was Jasper. Phoebe felt her pulse in her throat, as she actually caught a glimpse of him now that he wasn't wearing his baseball hat. His hair was dark brown and cut very short on the slides, but it was long and styled messily to the side on the top. His eyes were deep blue, and he had scruff on his face. He was ruggedly handsome. Phoebe could also see that he was an excellent dresser, just like Thomas. He was wearing grey pants and a light blue dress shirt, which was buttoned up higher than Thomas'. He had on brown shoes with a brown belt. Her eyes connected with Jasper. She looked away begging herself not to blush this time as he had caught her starring at him.

"Glad to see you guys could make it out," Anna said with her sweet smile that made everyone swoon over her, clearly it was having the same effect on Thomas.

"Yes, we promised my aunt that we would come today if she made us her famous cookies to go, which of course she did." Thomas laughed. He was so casual and happy. Phoebe could tell he was someone that she could be friends with right away; in fact, she couldn't see anyone not wanting to be friends with him. His personality was like a magnet within five seconds of meeting him. "You must be Wally," Thomas said turning to Phoebe.

"Wally?" Phoebe didn't understand. Fear that he had mistaken her for someone else pulsed through her body.

"Well, we haven't formally met, so Jasper and I decided that we would call you Wally, it's much nicer than Walrus." Anna burst out laughing so hard that she snorted. This time Phoebe could not control the colour of her face and felt it go tomato red. "I'm Thomas, people call me Tommy, and this is Jasper." He pointed to Jasper who was also chuckling. Phoebe tried to remain cool and not let her embarrassment take over.

"I'm Phoebe, although I do kind of like the name Wally." *Might as well go along with it,* she thought. Hopefully, it wouldn't seem like she wanted to crawl under a rock and hide even though she wanted to.

"It's nice to finally meet you, Phoebe." Jasper stuck of his hand to shake hers. As soon as she took his hand, she felt like she had been shocked. She had to look up to make eye contact with him, even in her three-inch heels. *He must be at least six-foot-five,* Phoebe thought. He continued to focus on her not taking his eyes off her and smiling. It felt like they were just starring at each other forever. *Did anyone else think so too?* Phoebe thought. *And why can't I look away?*

"Okay then…," Thomas had broken the trance with his voice. He looked between Jasper and Phoebe with a raised eyebrow.

"Oh, Jasper! I am so glad that you made it! I was hoping you would follow through with your promise to be here and sit with me!" Phoebe's hair stood up on the back of her neck. She knew that voice from anywhere. It was Brittany Mae. The most popular girl at their high school. She was basically like Anna but one thousand times meaner and power hungry. Brittany loved to remind Phoebe that she was nothing like Anna, and never would be, any chance she got. Phoebe didn't know what she had ever done to receive Brittany's domineering attention, but she felt like she always got it. Ever since grade nine, Brittany made it her mission to make sure Phoebe knew that she was "just average".

"Oh, hey, Anna, I didn't see you there. Wasn't last night so great? I feel like anyone who missed it will never understand how much fun we had. I could never explain all our little jokes. It's almost like it would just be our groups little secret." Brittany brushed her hair over her shoulder and batted her eyelashes a little more than needed. Phoebe could tell that this conversation was another way that Brittany was trying to show how insignificant Phoebe was.

"It was really fun, hopefully, we can do something like that again the next time we have HSCC." Anna smiled back oblivious to the hit Phoebe had just taken. The music started to play in the auditorium signalling the service was about to start.

"Come on, Jasper, you can't back out of your promise now!" Brittany pulled on Jasper's arm tugging him towards seats to the left. Anna and Phoebe were not invited to join them.

"See you Anderson ladies later." Thomas shrugged and followed his friend to their seats. Phoebe and Anna walked down closer to the front and sat with their mother. Phoebe could see Mary sitting next to Andrew and his mom. They usually sat with the Anderson's but when Andrew's mom didn't have to work at the hospital on a Sunday, they always sat with her. Phoebe tried to sing along with the songs that the band played and listen to Pastor Moore preach about John the Baptist, but her mind couldn't get away from thinking about Jasper. She didn't even know why. They had literally met for maybe five minutes, but her mind wouldn't stop thinking about his smile and the way he said her name. Phoebe wished that she could turn around and look at him and Brittany. *Were they interested in each other? Had they just met yesterday or before? Jasper must be interested in her if he promised that he would sit with her today.* Before Phoebe realized it, the church service was over. She felt horrible that she had barely heard a word that Pastor Moore had said. Shaking her head, she followed her mom and Anna into the main entrance.

"Phoebe, could you please go get Tabby from her classroom. I just want to talk with Mrs. Jones about something. I'll meet you girls by the van, so we can go out for lunch." Mrs. Anderson hustled through the crowd to find Mrs. Jones. Phoebe walked down the hall and had to almost pull Tabby physically from her classroom. All of her little friends were complimenting her on her lipstick. Tabby was beaming as they made their way outside to the front walkway.

"Did you have a good time?" Phoebe asked Tabby.

"Yes! Samantha couldn't believe that I was wearing this lipstick. I could tell that Jenny was so jealous. All the girls couldn't stop asking me what shade it was." Tabby was basically bouncing with joy.

"I am glad you feel beautiful, Tabby, but I hope you remember dad said you aren't allowed to wear it again and you are just as beautiful without it." Phoebe tried to gently remind her.

"I know, but it was so worth it." Tabby grinned up at Phoebe. Phoebe couldn't help but smile at her cunning little sister.

"Is this another little Anderson?" Phoebe whirled around to find Thomas and Jasper walking towards them.

"Hey, everyone," Phoebe smiled trying not to seem as excited and nervous as she felt. She noticed that Brittany was nowhere in sight. "This is my little sister, Tabitha."

"It's Tabby." Tabby stuck out her hip and put her hand on it. "Who are you guys." Jasper and Thomas both laughed at her aggressive approach.

"Hey, Tabby, I'm Thomas and this is Jasper." Thomas held out his hand to shake Tabby's. She shook it and smiled brightly up at him. She was clearly pulled in like a magnet just like the rest of them.

"Hey, guys!" Anna walked up to them. Thomas started to talk to Anna about Fendry College and the pep rally coming up. Tabby was trying to get Thomas' attention to fit into the conversation. Phoebe smiled at her little sister clearly smitten by the really friendly and really attractive Thomas.

"So, we are going to get some pizza now. Do you and your sister's want to come?" Jasper asked Phoebe, quietly pulling her attention from the rest of the group.

"Um, I would really like to, but my dad wants to take us out to lunch today. It's kind of a big deal. He never takes us all out to lunch. There are so many of us we can never agree on a place to go, and it usually costs a fortune." *Why am I blabbering and telling him this?* Phoebe thought. She looked at her high heels and tried to stop herself from rambling.

"Ok, cool. Maybe next time then." Phoebe looked back up at Jasper. He was so tall. He was starring right down into her eyes. His smile tilted up higher on the right side, but it made him even more endearing.

"I would really like that." Phoebe could feel her cheeks turning red again and willed them to stop.

"So, Anna said that you are finishing up your senior year and then are going to go to Fendry?" Jasper asked.

"That is if I get in. The program is really competitive. I am starting to get anxious waiting for my acceptance letter," Phoebe admitted. She didn't know why but she felt like she could be completely honest with Jasper, and he wouldn't judge her.

"I am sure you will get in. You seem like you take it pretty seriously. I mean you even missed a church event to study." Jasper smirked. Not in a way that made her feel bad, but it actually made her feel proud. "What program did you apply for?"

"Education. I would love to be a primary schoolteacher." Phoebe shrugged.

"That's really cool. I hope you get in. It would be nice to have another friendly face around campus." Jasper grinned at Phoebe.

"Thanks, I..." Phoebe got cut off by a cooing holler.

"Jaaaaasper!" Brittany came bounding out from the front church door. "Do you think you could give me a ride to the pizza place and then maybe one home? I came with my parents today since my car is in the shop?" Again, Brittany grabbed onto Jasper's arm and gave a cute little pout.

"Sure, I've got room." Jasper nodded back at her.

"Well, I am ready to go when you are." Brittany gave a playful little tug on his arm clearly pretending that Phoebe was not standing there. "Thomas, we are going to go now," Brittany said in a singsong voice.

"Well, I hope we see you young ladies around soon," Thomas said pretending to tip a fake hat to them. Tabby let out an obnoxious laugh. She was trying to flirt with him. Phoebe couldn't help but let out a little giggle for her sister's sake.

The Anderson girls waved good-bye. Phoebe could hear Brittany saying that she invited her friends to meet them at the pizza place and how Jasper would just love all her friends. A wave of jealously came over her. She wished she could have gone for pizza with Jasper instead of having to go to lunch with the family. Now Brittany got to spend more time with Jasper showing him how interesting and perfect she was. The first time a guy had actually asked her to go somewhere. Even though the invitation was as a friend. Phoebe didn't know why but that made the disappointment in her heart grow ten times bigger.

Chapter Five

The week felt like it was flying by to Phoebe. It was already Wednesday. All she had done was gone to classes, finished homework or go to work. She picked up an extra after school shift at the bakery because one of the other girls had called in sick. Phoebe didn't mind. She needed the extra money, but now she was really missing her friends, and even more so, the couch. All she wanted to do was finish packing up her backpack and go home to watch some mindless T.V.

"Jenn is looking for you," Maggie, one of Phoebe's best friend said, plopping her backpack on the floor beside Phoebe's locker. "She is freaking out."

"Why what happened?" Phoebe had barely talked to her friends so far this week. They had all managed to have lunch together on Monday where she told both of them about Jasper and their Walrus meeting. Maggie was on student council so that was taking up a lot of her time and Jenn was helping to design the costumes for the school play. Phoebe had tried to make Jasper seem like it wasn't anything big, just an embarrassing moment to share with her friends. However, she still couldn't shake Jasper's lopsided smile out of her mind.

"You'll see. Here she comes." Maggie pointed to a blur running towards them down the hall.

"Phoebe Anderson!" Jenn yelled with both anger and excitement. She stuck both hands on her hips.

"Jennifer?" Phoebe questioned and mimicked her best friend's stance.

"Why did you not tell me that Jasper was actually thee Jasper Brown from the Fendry Fire Hawks?" Jenn's voice came out as a loud squeak. The people across the hall stopped and looked at her strangely, then turned back around.

"Uh, maybe because I didn't know he was "thee" anything. What are you talking about?" Phoebe kept shoving books into her bag that Maggie was now holding out for her.

"Jasper Brown is THEE best player on Fendry! His batting average is out of this world and he is the best outfielder in the whole NCAA!"

"The NC what, what?" Phoebe stopped to look at Jenn's whose face was beet red with excitement.

"It's the National Collegiate Athletics Association." Jenn rolled her eyes. Phoebe looked to Maggie to see if she knew what Jenn was talking about. Maggie just shrugged. "Your Jasper is already being scouted to move up to the big leagues! How did you not know this?"

"First of all, he is not my Jasper. We met twice, and if you remember I'd rather forget the first time," Phoebe said laughing along with her two best friends as they recalled the walrus meeting. "I didn't know how good he was. It's not like it came up in conversation and I don't follow sports like you do."

"Well, maybe, you should start," Jenn said crossing her arms over the chest.

A locker door slammed near the girls making them all jump.

"Jasper said he might call me this week and let me know if he is going to church again on Sunday. He said he and Thomas can't make it every weekend because of the games, but he wants to try and go as much as he can." Brittany was speaking very loudly to Charlotte and Laura a couple lockers down the hall from Phoebe and her friends. "Wasn't he so funny? I definitely think he is interested in me. I mean he did offer to take me home and you heard him say he was so happy I came out with them." Maggie and Jenn looked at Phoebe and winced. Phoebe didn't want to look at them because she knew it would be a look of pity. How could she ever compete with head cheerleader Brittany? "Thomas is so cool too. I really think you and Thomas could hit it off, Charlotte. Next time we go out, I'll help you pick out an outfit." Brittany slammed her locker door and passed Phoebe in the hall. Her friends walking behind her. She turned around and looked at Phoebe smugly as if to say, "he's mine".

"That was... interesting." Maggie said trying to break the silence.

"Like, I said. He isn't my Jasper. He did seem pretty friendly with Brittany at church. Sorry, Jenn, if you want an autograph, you'll have to ask her." Phoebe shut the door to her locker and said a quick good-bye to her friends. Her need to go under a blanket on the couch grew tenfold. She tried to hide it from her friends, but she was hurt. Her crush on Jasper Brown would clearly stay just a crush.

****

"Pheebs? Honey? Is that you?" Phoebe's mom called from the kitchen.

"Yup. Hi, mom." Phoebe called back, placing the car keys into the bowl on the table by the door. She dropped her schoolbag on the first step and walked into the kitchen to find her mom baking cupcakes. Phoebe reached out to grab one.

"Don't you dare!" Phoebe mom said, pretending to swat her hand away playfully. "Those are for Tabby's class tomorrow. They are having a party for winning the best class science project." Phoebe put a big pout on her face and batted her eyelashes. "Oh fine. Just one though!"

"Thanks, Mom! She grabbed a big fat cupcake and turned to go lay on the couch.

"Phoebe, don't get too comfortable. I actually need you to pick up Anna from cheer practice. I can't make it because of these cupcakes and your dad is stuck on the job site."

"Mom, I really just want to stay home. I can do the rest of the cupcakes for you." Phoebe looked pleadingly at her mom.

"Nope, you wanted to take the car to school today, you get to pick up the person you share the car with. I would make Anna pick up you too, if the positions were reversed."

"Fine." Phoebe shoved the warm cupcake in her mouth. "When do I have to leave?" Some of the crumbs came flying out of her mouth at her mother.

"Ew, Phoebe!" Her mother tried to say seriously but ended up laughing. "You have to leave in 10 minutes. She said to meet her out on the lower bleachers. That way you can find each other, and she isn't searching all of the parking lots.

"Alright, I am just going to go change. I feel so gross and tired."

"Thank you, I will make you a to-go coffee. Now hurry up." Her mother shooed her up the stairs. She quickly changed into her favourite ripped jeans and comfy camo sweater. Phoebe pulled up her hair into a high ponytail and slip on some cherry lip gloss. Much better, she thought. Now at least she felt a bit more like herself. Her mom had placed the to-go mug on the table by the door.

"Thanks, Mom!" Phoebe called as she headed at the door.

"Just be back in time for dinner!" Mrs. Anderson called out.

The drive to Fendry College only took twenty minutes from Phoebe's house. It was an easy drive on the highway. Phoebe had Christian rock blaring on the car radio, and she drummed her fingers on the steering wheel to the beat. She found a parking spot by the sports field. Hopping out of the car and locking the door she walked over to the bleachers. It looked like the cheerleaders were just finishing up their meeting. Phoebe sometimes wished that she would have tried out for cheerleading like Anna had begged her to when she started high school, but Phoebe knew it wasn't her thing. She would have done it for the wrong reasons. Her dad had always said to only do activities that she enjoyed and that would help her bring joy to the Lord. She knew Anna and cheerleading were made for that, not her and cheerleading. She liked working her job at the bakery and using that money to take care of herself. She liked being with kids and helping them understand or learn new things. Self-discovery is hard.

Phoebe heard a whoop from down the field and saw a bunch of guys doing sprints. She squinted her eyes to try and make out what team they were. The coach stood up from the bleachers and blew his whistle signalling the players to come join him. The back of his jacket said, "Fire Hawks Baseball". Phoebe's heart skipped a beat. She started to scan all the players hustling their way back to the coach. They were all wearing baseball caps, so it was hard to see any of their faces this far away. She leaned forward on the bleachers trying to get a better look.

"Whatcha looking at?" came a snicker from in front of Phoebe. It was Anna with her pom-poms on her hips grinning slyly at her.

"For you..." Phoebe said, sitting back on the cold metal seat.

"Come one Pheebs, you don't have to lie to me. Jasper is number fifteen. Unless it's Thomas you are looking for then he is number twenty-three."

"No, I'm not." Phoebe shook her head trying to think of a better reason that she would be peering over at the baseball guys.

"Ha-ha! It's fine, Pheebs. They are really nice guys. Out of all of them on the team they are both Christians and not afraid to show it. Which is super rare if you know what I mean? I have to go get changed but I will meet you right here as soon as I am done. I'll try to be fast."

"Okay," was all Phoebe could mutter. What had gotten into her? She never would be shy to tell her sister anything, especially Anna. She was usually the one that understood her the most. First, because she was the most compassionate out of the family, but also because she was closest to Phoebe in age. Anna gave Phoebe a knowing grinned and turned to go get changed out of her cheer uniform. Her light brown ponytail was bouncing behind her. The closer she got to the locker room entrance a bunch of the baseball guys all turned and called her name. She responded to their hellos with a cute wave of her pom-poms. When she entered the locker room door, she could see all the guys punch each other and laughing, probably so excited that they had gotten Anna's attention. Phoebe wished that she had gotten that kind of attention from guys, but she usually felt invisible compared to Anna.

"Hey, Phoebe, I thought that was you." Phoebe gave a little jump from the deep voice from in front of the bleacher fence. Jasper was leaning on the fence. His eyes were shadowed by the brim of his red and black baseball cap, but his lopsided smile was beaming at her.

"Hey, Jasper." She tried to act casual. She didn't think it was working.

"I saw you sitting up here, when I was doing sprints. I thought I'd come say hi. So, hi." Was it just Phoebe or did he sound a bit nervous too.

"Ha-ha, Hi. I am here to pick up Anna from cheer. We share a car, and I needed it for school today, so I had to come pick her up." Why did she always have to ramble on when she talked to him?

"Right." Jasper nodded his head. He looked like he was trying to think of something to say too. "We usually aren't on this field. The diamond is actually over there." He pointed to his left. Phoebe looked and could see the baseball diamond further down beyond the football field. "Today, coach wanted to do conditioning and the football field has the yards mapped out, so it works the best."

"That makes sense." *Come on Phoebe, think of something better to say.*

"So, how has your week been?" Jasper asked. Why couldn't Phoebe have thought to ask that? She felt like she couldn't stop starring at his crooked smile and scruff covered square jaw.

"It's actually been really busy. Between work and school, I feel like I haven't done much of anything. I am really looking forward to the weekend." Phoebe was finally starting to relax. She remembered how easy it was to talk to Jasper on Sunday.

"I hear ya on that one. Tommy and I are going to help out his aunt again this weekend. She is trying to do some work on her backyard. Right now, we are demoing it for her." Phoebe felt her heart leap a little. Did that mean he was going to come to church again? "We are thinking about driving out after our Friday game. Hey, would you and your sister want to grab some breakfast on Saturday?" Jasper leaned on the fence. He looked so casual and relaxed.

"Did I hear someone say breakfast? That's my favourite meal of the day!" Thomas walked up behind Jasper with two other guys from the team.

"You like every meal man; I am sure that's one of the reasons Coach made us do conditioning today. You like your meals a little too much." One of the other guys said. Phoebe recognized him from the mall; he was the blonde on his phone, but she didn't know who the other guy was. He had dark chocolate skin with a small goatee on his chin. The goatee guy fist bumped the blonde and they both laughed. Thomas rubbed his stomach and grinned.

"A guy has got to eat." He smiled unaffected by their words. "Hey, Wally, I was wondering who Jasper was talking to over here."

"Hey, Tommy," Phoebe nodded back to him. Thomas grinned at the fact that she used his nickname as well. Phoebe actually didn't mind being called Wally, coming from Thomas she knew he meant it in a friendly way.

"So, this is Wally!" The goatee guy exclaimed and came close to the fence. Jasper turned to face him and the goatee guy and immediately shut his mouth. Phoebe wondered what the exchange of non-verbal communication was about.

"Wally or I also go by Phoebe or Pheebs," Phoebe said giving a smile. She felt like she could relax now that it wasn't just her and Jasper talking, although a part of her wished it was.

"I'm Parker," said the goatee guy, "and this is Leo." He slapped the blond on his back. Leo just nodded his chin at Phoebe, still not saying anything.

"So, what is this about breakfast?" Tommy asked looking back to Jasper.

"I was just telling her that we are helping out your aunt again this weekend, so we would be in Hillwood. I didn't know if her, Anna and her other sisters wanted to grab some breakfast on Saturday."

"Wait, your Anna's little sister? Count me in for breakfast on Saturday," Parker said now leaning closer in on the fence. *So, he was one of Anna's many admirers*, Phoebe thought.

"Thanks for the invited but I can't," Phoebe explained.

"Whoa, dude, you just got turned down!" Parker punched Jasper in the arm laughing. Phoebe wasn't sure why it was so funny.

"I actually work early on Saturday mornings," She explained.

"Where do you work?" Thomas asked. It seemed like he was trying to defuse some of the tension that Parker was creating. Although, Phoebe wasn't sure why it was such a big deal, he had asked to go in a group. He wasn't asking her on a date, was he? No way he could be.

"At Barker's Bakery. I do the morning prep every Saturday. It's really early in the morning, but I love it." Phoebe shrugged her shoulders.

"Barker's Bakery! I love that place. Last weekend we got some of the cinnamon bread there and it was amazing!" Thomas exclaimed. "Wait, do you make it?" He put his hands on his heart dramatically.

"I do, actually." Phoebe grinned at how passionate he was being.

"No way! I think you just became my favourite new person. How come I didn't see you there last week?" Thomas asked.

"I start work at 5:30 and finish at 12:00. I am in the back doing the prep and baking, so I don't usually deal with customers on Saturdays. I only work the front after school a couple times a week."

"Hey, guys," Anna said, walking up the bleacher and sitting down next to Phoebe. Phoebe could see Parker and Leo, who had been not interested in the conversation before, perk up. "I see you've found my little sister," she said, giving Phoebe a wink. Phoebe felt her cheeks heating up.

"That was a really cool pyramid you guys were working on today." Thomas made a triangle out of his hands.

"Thanks, it's pretty tricky, but I think we will get it." Anna smiled at all of them. "Well, Pheebs, we need to get going. Mom just called me and asked if we were on our way home yet."

"Okay," Phoebe said starting to get up.

"Maybe, we will see you guys at church on Sunday again?" Thomas pushed himself back and forth hanging onto the fence.

"That sounds good." Anna flashed them all a smile and picked up her cheer bag. "By the way you guys looked really good out there today."

"Some more than others," Parker said, flashing her a big smile. It kind of made Phoebe feel a little uncomfortable.

"Come on, man," Leo grabbed Parker by the shirt and started to drag him away. Thomas and Jasper turned to go too, but Phoebe caught Jasper giving her a small wave in the corner of her eye, while turning around. She smiled at him and gave a small wave back. Phoebe followed Anna to the car.

"So, what was that all about?" Anna asked, giving Phoebe an impish grin.

"Jasper asked if we could have breakfast with them on Saturday morning. I guess they are helping out Thomas' Aunt again. She is redoing her backyard."

Phoebe shrugged trying to make it seem like it wasn't a big deal, even though she was freaking out. She was so excited that Jasper had actually noticed her.

"Wow, that was nice of them. What did you say?"

"I told them we couldn't because I had to work, but I should have said you guys could have made it. Sorry, I am sure you could catch up with them and let them know." Phoebe felt bad that she forgot to mention that to the guys.

"It's fine, Pheebs. Plus, I don't think Jasper was really asking if I could go." Anna raised her eyebrows at Phoebe as they pulled out of the school parking lot.

"Leo and Parker seemed to only be interested when they heard you would be there," Phoebe replied. *Did Jasper really ask because he had wanted to hang out with her?* Then it hit Phoebe and she felt her heart drop. What if Jasper was asking because he wanted to see Anna. Phoebe was an easy way to gain access to her older sister. She could recall more than once a guy who had used Phoebe to hang out with Anna.

"Those two aren't exactly my type." Anna waved her hand in the air. The rest of the car ride home Phoebe remained quiet as Anna sang along to the songs. She felt her heart sinking deeper and deeper in her chest. Jasper must be one of Anna's admirers. No matter how hard she tried to convince herself to let it go. Her crush only grew deeper, and her self-confidence was taking a hit.

Chapter Six

The rest of the week had flown by just like the first half. Phoebe was so glad when the bell rang on Friday afternoon signalling it was time to go home.

"Thank God for the weekend. Seriously, thank Him because I need rest! I thought the last half of senior year was supposed to be fun and less work," Jenn said slumping down on the floor beside Phoebe's locker. Maggie, Jenn, and Phoebe always met at Phoebe's locker at the end of the day. Sometimes they were so busy with clubs or work that the end of the day was the only time they got to talk to one another.

"Agreed, Anna told me once April hits, teachers start to lessen their assignment load. I think the teachers have to get one last report in for some colleges before then." Phoebe grabbed her books and plunked them in her backpack. "You know what we should do? We should plan a girls' night like we use to have. Movies, nail polish, and snacks!"

"Yes! I can't this weekend, though, my dad wants us to go visit my Abeula." Jenn opened up her planner. "Next weekend works, though."

"Maggie! Next weekend girls' night?" Phoebe clapped her hands and jumped as Maggie met them.

"That should work for me. I might have to stay a bit later after school, since we're organizing for Prom and setting up the nomination process for Prom King and Queen. But I could meet you guys after that?"

"Yay!" Jenn and Phoebe grabbed Maggie jumping up and down. Maggie didn't join in. She was too professional to act like a little girl in public. Phoebe knew they could crack open that side of her next weekend, though.

"I just came to say a quick hello and good-bye. I have to help cut out the ballots for the prom theme vote." Maggie always surprised Phoebe. She was a feminist and big into politics, but then she could be so excited about things like prom even if she didn't let it show. "Have you guys decided what you want to vote for. Of course, you don't have to tell me. You have the right to privacy." Maggie held out her hand as if to say stop.

"I think I want it to be it be masquerade," Jenn said excited. "I think it would be a true display of creativity and design on the part of our class. I decided, I am going to make my own dress for prom. I have been toying with a few ideas for all potential themes, but I am really enjoying the masquerade theme the best." Jenn's two favourite things: sports and fashion. Of course, she would be designing her own dress. Phoebe could not wait to see it.

"I don't really have a preference," Phoebe admitted.

"I think I will vote black and white. There is just something so classic about it," Maggie sighed. "Okay, I have to get going. I will call you guys later!" Maggie ran off back down the hall to help the other student council members with the prom ballots.

"I have to go too. I promised my dad I would be ready to leave when I got home from school, but I haven't even packed for the weekend yet. I'll try to call you from my Abeula's." Jenn stood up and gave Phoebe a quick hug before she hustled back through the crowded halls too. Phoebe picked up her bag, heaved it over her shoulder and was ready to head home for a nap.

It was College and Careers' Friday night at the church, so Phoebe was staying home again; but to her surprise Anna and Mary decided to stay home too. Andrew was sick so he didn't come over. They decided to watch The Princess Bride with Tabby, another one of the Anderson's staple movies. Tabby still closed her eyes during the scarier parts. Phoebe had to admit that she closed her eye too when they were sucking the life out of Wesley. It had been a long time since just the four of them had had an Anderson sister night. It was exactly what Phoebe needed and since Tabby still had a bedtime, they all went to bed early.

The next morning Phoebe woke up feeling refreshed and ready to go, which was basically a miracle with how run down she had been feeling and that it was 5:00 in the morning. She quickly did her usual morning routine. Thankfully, Anna didn't need the car today, so she took a little bit more time on her makeup. She pulled up her hair in a ponytail and wore a pink sweater and jeans. Quietly walking downstairs and out the door as to not wake anyone else in the family, Phoebe looked at the clock. She was going to be right on time for bakery prep.

Mrs. Barker's car was already there when Phoebe pulled into the parking spaces behind the bakery. She quickly hopped out and headed into the store using her key. Phoebe wondered what time Mrs. Barker got there. She always seemed to be the first one there and the last one out not matter what time of day it was. Mrs. Barker must really love owning and running the bakery. One of Phoebe's goals in life was to love her job. This was something that really worried her and even scared her because she still hadn't found her true passion. She wanted to be a teacher right now, but she hoped that when she actually was teaching it would bring her joy. She wanted to be more confident in herself and her life choices such as her career. It stressed he out thinking of the future. When Phoebe walked into the store, the sweet smells of pastries wafted through the air. Mrs. Barker was already in the back putting this weekend's specials into the oven. It was banana bread, but the secret was the icing that they pour on top of it when it was still warm. It created a sweet sugary glaze. It was one of Phoebe's favourites.

"Morning, Mrs. Barker. How are you?" Phoebe asked as he put her items away and got ready to help with the prep.

"Just great, doll. How are you?" Mrs. Baker closed the door of the oven and walked over to a counter, handing Phoebe one of the coffee cups that sat there. "I want you to try this and tell me what you think." Phoebe sipped from the steamy cup. She gave a groan of satisfaction.

"What is that?" she asked Mrs. Barker.

"Oh, good. I like it too and so did Mr. Barker; but us old coots are sometimes off our rockers. I had to make sure someone from your generation would enjoy it as well. Its coffee infused with walnuts and a little bit of caramel. I thought of it in my sleep two nights ago and I think I finally nailed it. I wanted to serve it with the banana bread today."

"It's amazing and definitely the perfect match for the bread." Phoebe took another delicious sip.

"I am going to go make sure a carafe is full of it then. Can you continue with the bread? I have a feeling today is going to be a busy one. I want to make sure everything is set to go." Mrs. Barker turned and headed out front to set up the coffee station. *Mrs. Barker must really love this place if she dreams of new creations,* Phoebe thought.

The morning passed by quickly and Mrs. Barker was correct. The store was super busy today. Phoebe ended up making twice the amount of banana bread than usually to keep up with the demand. Everyone was raving about the new coffee Mrs. Barker had come up with. Phoebe was about to get ready to leave for the day when Dani, one of the other girls who ran the counter, came out back.

"Hey, Phoebe, there is someone out front asking if you are still here."

"Okay, thanks; I'll be right there." Phoebe thought it was probably Maggie coming in and trying to get a free coffee. Sometimes, she did that when she was passing through town and wanted to say hi. Phoebe decided that she should grab her stuff and bring it out front to grab a coffee and some banana bread with Maggie before heading home. When she walked out from the backroom, Dani pointed to one of the small round tables to the left. There wasn't much room in the bakery for tables so they were small and only two people could fit at them. There, making one of the tables look ten times smaller, was Jasper. Phoebe's pulse quickened as she walked over to the table. Dani gave her two thumbs up and appeared to mouth "wow" to her as she walked away.

"Hey," Phoebe tried to say loud and friendly, but it came out more as a squeak.

"Hey, Phoebe, I was just at the hardware store and thought I'd get some of that cinnamon bread for Thomas. He couldn't stop talking about it. Jasper had on a pair of ripped jeans, a plaid jacket, and a plain black baseball cap. It looked like he had shaved this morning, so his scruff was gone. He smiled his lopsided smile at Phoebe. Her heart melted.

"Oh, well, I am really sorry, but the special today is banana bread, so we don't have any of the cinnamon. I can promise you though that the banana bread is just as amazing, and Mrs. Barker made this delicious walnut infused coffee to go with it," Phoebe said, still standing in front of the table. She wasn't sure if she should sit down or if she should just keep standing.

"That sounds great. I'll take two loaves and two coffees." Jasper nodded his head to Phoebe.

"Oh, sure. One second." Phoebe got up and told Dani the order. Jasper followed her to the front glass counter and paid for the items.

"Here you go, handsome," Dani winked at Jasper handing him back his change and passed over the coffees. Phoebe shook her head. Dani felt no shame. She would flirt with anyone that came into the store. They weren't exactly friends, but they were not unfriendly. Dani liked to party a lot and since that wasn't Phoebe's scene, nor was she allowed to go to those kinds of parties, they had never really bonded.

"Here, this one is for you." Jasper passed Phoebe one of the coffee's he bought.

"Thanks, you didn't have to do that." Phoebe grinned taking the coffee.

"Well, since I didn't get to buy you breakfast the other day, I can at least get you a coffee." Phoebe's heart did a flip. Did he actually mean he wanted the breakfast to be a date? She tried to regain the control of her nerves. She took a sip of the hot sweet drink, so did Jasper. "Wow, this really is amazing." Jasper looked down into his cup, surprised.

"You will have to try it with a slice of the bread later. Like I said it is one of my favourites, I promise you won't be sorry."

"I'll take you word for it." He smiled back at her; Phoebe caught a glimpse of his eyes under his hat. They had a sparkle to them. Jasper opened the front door letting Phoebe walk in front of him and followed. "Can I walk you to your car?"

"Sure, um, it's just around back." They started to walk around the building in silence. *Think of something to say!* Phoebe screamed in her head.

"How is Mrs. Hernandez's backyard coming? You said you guys were demoing it?"

"Yeah, it's going slower than I thought. We don't really have the right equipment for it, but it is a great work out." Jasper shrugged.

"There must be a lot to pull out if all four of you are still working on it."

"It's just me and Thomas doing it. Leo and Parker don't want to come because we decide to stay and go to church, they don't like that," Jasper explained openly.

"Oh." Phoebe wasn't sure how to respond.

"We are going to church again tomorrow, though. Are you guys having a family lunch again?" They had finally got to Phoebe's car, standing by the driver side door.

"No, not that I know of."

"Would you want to go for pizza with us. We usually grab some before we head back to Fendry; and I'll be honest with how much Thomas eats we usually buy a box with for the car ride too," Jasper smirked.

"Wow, he really can eat."

"That's why I got two loaves of bread." Jasper held up the bag containing the loaves that Dani had packed in it. He was silent and Phoebe remembered that she still hadn't answered his question.

"I would have to clear it with my dad, but I am sure it would be fine to grab a couple of slices. I'll mention it to Anna too."

"Cool. Tabby can come too if she wants." He gave a shrug. Phoebe knew he was being completely genuine in saying that Tabby could come. She didn't know whether to think that was sweet or be disappointed. At least, he didn't make it seem like he just wanted Anna to come.

"Ok, I'll talk to my sisters and dad tonight." Phoebe smiled back at him. She really hoped that her dad would let her go. He was really strict when it came to going out with people he didn't know, especially boys. But she hoped since he knew of Thomas' aunt and Anna knew them from school, he would let them.

"Great." Jasper put down his bag of bread and grabbed his phone out of his plaid coat pocket. "Why don't you give me your phone number and I'll text you my name, that way you can let me know?" Phoebe gave him her phone number and he said he would text her when he got back to Thomas' aunt's house. Phoebe climbed into her car and waved good-bye. She couldn't get the smile off her face. It was beginning to feel like Jasper was actually asking her out, even if her sisters were invited too. At least that is what she was hoping for.

When Phoebe pulled into the driveway of her house, she heard a ding go off on her phone. She turned off the car and took the keys out of the ignition. Looking down at her cell phone, she saw it was from an unknown number all it said was "Jasper Brown".

Chapter Seven

Phoebe walked into her house ready to go up and just ask her dad about grabbing pizza with Jasper and Thomas after church tomorrow. *It wasn't that big of a deal, right? Her sisters were invited too, even Tabby.* She marched into the kitchen where she could hear her mom in conversation with her dad.

"Oh, I am so sorry, John, there isn't any company that can help with the tow?" Her mom asked as Phoebe turned the corner. It turned out that she was talking to Phoebe's dad on the phone. Phoebe felt some of her confidence fade away. Her mom noticed her and mouth that she would be off in a second. "Okay, sweetie, just be safe and I will see you when you come home. Love you too." Phoebe's mom put the phone down on the counter and sighed. "Hi, dear, how was work this morning?"

"It was good. Mrs. Barker made this amazing new coffee blend. I wanted to bring some home, but they were selling out of it so fast." Phoebe took a deep breath trying to not lose all of her courage. "Mom, will Dad be home soon?"

"I am afraid not. One of the new guys accidentally backed up the loader into the client's pond and it's sinking. Your father is trying to get it out before it is completely flooded, but all of the towing companies are closed already." Phoebe's dad owned and ran a landscaping company called Anderson's Care. He had started it up when her parents were just dating, and it continually grew and grew. Phoebe knew how hard her dad had worked and how upset he would be that his machine might be ruined.

"That's not good," Phoebe said, starting to bite her nails. "A friend stopped by the bakery today and asked if we could go out for pizza after church with him and his friends." Phoebe tried to sound like it was no big deal, but she knew in her heart that it was a pretty big deal to her.

"Well, I am not sure, Phoebe. Do I know this boy? And who was he asking to go, just you?"

"I don't think you have met him before. His name is Jasper Brown; Anna knows him. He and Thomas Hernandez play baseball for Fendry. Thomas is Mrs. Hernandez's nephew."

"Oh, Alison was mentioning that her nephew was helping her out at her house on some weekends." Her mom was bustling around the kitchen putting away dishes. Phoebe wished she would just stop for a second so they could finish their conversation. Her heart was beating so fast, thinking about the possibility of spending more time with Jasper even if it was with a big group of people including her ten-year-old little sister.

"He asked if Mary and Anna could come too. He even said Tabby could come." Mrs. Anderson continued to hustle around the kitchen and Phoebe tried to move out of her path every time she came close. She knew from past experience that when her mom was stressed out, she usually needed to keep cleaning or cooking to keep her mind off whatever was bothering her.

"That sounds really nice, dear, just mention it to your dad later, if it isn't too late when he gets home." That was not the answer that Phoebe was hoping for. She wanted her mom just to say they could go. Her dad would most likely be frustrated and not want to talk about anything when he came home from dealing with work issues, especially as big as a sinking machine. Phoebe's mom was too busy hustling around moving things to noticed that she backed out of the kitchen. Phoebe head upstairs to take a hot shower to get some of the bakery smells and leftover ingredients off herself.

When Phoebe had finished in the shower, she decided that she should take the time and pamper herself a little. She had smeared on vanilla body cream and painted her toes and fingers nails in a soft pale pink. She had blown dried her hair out which gave more body to her long brown locks. She had even taken on the task of plucking her eyebrows, something she hated doing but was very happy she had decided to after she saw that a little unibrow was forming. By the time she was done, she could hear commotion coming from downstairs. She glanced at her clock and saw that it was nearly 3:00pm. Her sisters must be home from wherever they had gone this morning. Sometimes, Phoebe was jealous that her sisters were able to go out on Saturdays, but she knew that she appreciated having money to save or spend better. She went to go see what was happening.

"Well, hello, little sister." Anna gave Phoebe a fancy queen like wave as she saw her coming down the stairs. "We were just trying to coax mom into doing a girls' night with us. You would grace us with your presence, yes?" Anna's contagious smile lured Phoebe in.

"Of course," Phoebe responded, trying to put on her best British accent. "What did you have in mind?"

"Well, we are going to order pizza and rent some chick flicks and do all sorts of slumber party activities, such as painting our nails, which I can see you just did, nice colour. Maybe we would also do each other's hair, nice blow out too. We could conclude by picking out our outfits for church tomorrow... or did you already have that done as well?" Anna gave her a knowing kind of glance. Phoebe could tell she knew something was up because Phoebe hardly ever gave herself pamper days.

"No, I haven't done that, but I would be delighted for the help." Phoebe continued the charade.

"Fantastic, darling, come and tell the others." Phoebe linked arms with Anna. She was so lucky to be close with her sisters. So many people couldn't believe how well they had all gotten along, especially, because of how different they all were.

"I have just told Pheebs here about our evening plans and she is going to join our little extravaganza. Now, you have to join Mother, or you will be letting us all down." Anna gave their mom a pleading look and a tiny wink to Tabby, who was now giggling and jumping up and down.

"Fine, fine. I doubt your dad won't be home until later anyways. I will join your extravaganza," Mrs. Anderson waved her hand in the air, mimicking Anna, "but, only until he comes home."

"Yay!" All of the Anderson sisters cheered. Tabby and Anna grabbed hands and twirled around the room.

"Anna, you should really take a drama class next year. You have such a knack for it," Mary said, pulling open the take-out menu drawer. "I heard that Fendry actually has a really sought-after drama program." Mary was always trying to get her sisters to explore options, particularly Anna. Anna was in school for cosmetology, for some reason Mary always suggested she should try something else. Phoebe thought Anna would be amazing at hairdressing and makeup, she never understood what Mary had against it.

"Well, thank you, darling," Anna bowed, "but I like to leave my theatrics exclusively for you dear sisters." Anna grabbed Tabby's hand and pulled her out of the kitchen. Phoebe could hear them bounding up the stairs, probably to grab all the essentials of girls' night.

"Mom, don't you think Anna should try something new? She is wasting her college experience by not even trying something. She needs to challenge herself. All she does is hair, makeup, and cheer." Mary found the pizza special menu and started to open it.

"Mary, your sister has found something that she enjoys doing. You need to support her in that and be happy for her."

"She could do something so much better for herself. She is so creative. I hate to see her standing behind a chair all day and not really be able to express herself artistically." Phoebe started to wish she had gone upstairs with Anna and Tabby. She had never heard Mary talk about Anna like she was disappointed with her before. Phoebe wondered what Mary actually thought of her.

"That's enough, Mary. God blessed Anna with artistic skills, yes. It is up to her to choose her path, just like you have chosen yours." Phoebe could tell that was the end of the conversation. Mary wasn't going to push her mom anymore. Her mom was going to continue to stand her ground. "Phoebe, why don't you go pick out some movie options?" Phoebe was glad her mom had given her a way out of tension filled room. With everything that just happened, now was not the time to bring up lunch with Jasper tomorrow to her sisters. Maybe, something had happened this morning that she was not aware of. Hopefully, once the girls' night festivities started the mood would change and she could bring it up again. Maybe, Anna could even tell their mom how nice Jasper and

Thomas both were. Phoebe picked out several chick flick options. All lighthearted in hopes that it would create a positive atmosphere.

Girls' night had not gone as Phoebe or any of the Anderson sisters had planned. It started out fine with them sitting around the dinner table, painting each other's nails talking about colours and interesting nail designs they had seen in magazines. When Anna had mentioned she was going to be learning about gel applications and nail shaping at school soon it was all the Mary needed to start hounding her about trying other classes at school. Anna did not handle it as gracefully as she did earlier, and an argument ensued. In efforts to ease the tension, Mrs. Anderson had them take out plates for dinner. When the pizza came, Phoebe's dad arrived home at the same time. He was covered from head to toe in stinky sludge and mud. Her mom had followed him downstairs to their master suite and they had not come back upstairs. That was three hours ago. Mary had also retreated upstairs to her shared room with Anna with a couple slices of pizza, saying she needed to work on a paper for one of her classes. That left Anna, Tabby, and Phoebe watching Miss Congeniality on the couch. Tabby's soft snores started to float through the air.

"I really do enjoy doing hair and make-up, you know. I think I am actually really good at it," Anna stated out of thin air. She didn't even move her gaze from the T.V.

"You are really good at it, Anna, and if you like it that's even better." Phoebe wasn't sure what to say. Usually, she was the one going to Anna for advice.

"Thanks, Pheebs. It just makes me think of the parable of the talents. I was actually just reading it the other day." Phoebe knew the parable Anna was talking about. Jesus told the story of a landowner who was going away and gave three of his servants different amounts of money or talents as the bible says. Two of the servants went and made even more money using what the landowner had given them, but one had dug a hole in the ground and buried his in fear. When the landowner returned, he celebrated the two who had grown what they had been given, but was very angry with the one who did nothing with his talents.

"Okay," Phoebe said, hoping her sister would explain what she was thinking.

"God has given us all different talents or gifts. It is not how much or what gift he has given us that really matters. It is what we do with our gift. I could use the opportunity of giving a manicure to witness, or I could show God's love by giving a homeless man a free haircut. I know Mary wants what is best for me, but I am not her. I don't want to be some high-stake career woman. That is just not me. I want to cheer as long as I can, get a place in a nice salon, start a family, be happy, and share the gospel." Anna finally looked over and shrugged at Phoebe.

"That sounds really great. If you know you want that, then you should do it."

"I will." Anna nodded her head and looked back at the screen.

"I wish I knew what God's talents for me were," Phoebe confessed. She had never really admitted that to anyone before. Her whole family knew she wasn't sure what she was good at yet, but she had never mentioned that it really bothered her.

"You will discover it. Sometimes, it takes people longer than others and that is okay. God will reveal it to you, you just have to ask." Anna gave her a bright smile as Tabby let out an even louder snore. Both Anna and Phoebe let out a quiet giggle. "If you can't figure it out, you can always come work at a salon with me. You did a really good job on your own nails," Anna said, clearly trying to lighten the mood from a heavy topic. "You want to explain why you gave yourself a little pampering today? You look nice, but we both know that is completely out of the ordinary for you." Phoebe was hoping that she would get away with not disclosing the real reason. She knew that when her dad got home from work today, the odds of her being able to have lunch with Jasper tomorrow were going down the drain. Wishful thinking, she still hadn't texted him back yet in hopes she could mention it to her dad in the morning. Phoebe decided to just tell Anna anyway. One, because Anna always knew when Phoebe was lying and two, she wanted her to come to lunch and to back her up with their parents.

"Jasper came into work this morning to buy some bread for him and Thomas. He asked if we could grab some pizza with them after church tomorrow." She felt her face betray her as it started going red.

"Well, that makes a lot of sense now," Anna said with and "I knew it" smirk. "Did you get the okay from mom and dad?"

"I asked mom, but you know her. She told me I had to talk to dad, and I haven't had the chance, obviously." Phoebe nodded to the door that led downstairs to her parents' room. "I was hoping, maybe, you could help me bring it up tomorrow?" Phoebe gave her sister a pleading smile.

"Okay. Listen, I will help you tomorrow and I will go to pizza, but…" Anna paused, "big sister moment coming… I have to admit I don't really know a lot about Jasper or Thomas. I know that they are super nice guys, and everyone likes them. They say they are Christians, but I haven't been around them much to know whether they act it or not. Do you get what I am saying? College jocks are a lot different than high school jocks. I just don't want you to get your hopes up or expect anything." Phoebe felt her stomach sink a little. She knew Anna wasn't trying to burst her bubble, but still Phoebe was hoping that Jasper might be a little interested in her.

"I get it." She nodded to Anna hoping that her sister couldn't see her inner thoughts. Tabby let out a louder snore.

"I think we should get her up to bed before she really starts going. I don't blame you for wanting your own room." Anna lifted Tabby up from the couch. Tabby's head laid on her shoulder as her arms hung like dead-weights. Phoebe turned off the movie and all of the remaining lights that were on. She led the way upstairs to help Anna get Tabby into bed.

It was an easy transfer and Tabby never woke up as they pulled the blankets up over her body.

"You know you can come sleep with me if you want." Phoebe nodded at Anna and Mary's shared room door.

"No, that's okay. Mary is probably already asleep, but by the off chance she isn't and starts in on me again, I will be taking you up on that offer." Anna gave Phoebe a quick hug and then disappeared into the dark bedroom. Phoebe shuffled to her bed, not realizing how tired she was. Glancing at the alarm clock on her bedside table she couldn't believe it was only ten o'clock. It felt like it should be much later. She grabbed her phone to plug it into the charger and noticed that there was a text message waiting.

Jasper: Hey Phoebe. Tommy and I had to go back to campus tonight. Coach said there was some sort of team meeting. Rain check on the pizza. Sorry.

Phoebe felt her heart sink a little. She sighed and realized it was most likely for the best, since she never got a chance to talk to her dad. With the tension between Mary and Anna tonight, lunch tomorrow with the both of them would likely be a disaster. She decided to send a quick message back to Jasper, but she didn't want to let him know she was going to have to cancel anyways.

Phoebe: No problem. Hope everything is okay with the team.

She was going to tell him that she would definitely take a rain check, but then she felt it seems like she was being pushy or something, so she erased it and pressed send. She was definitely disappointed, but she also felt relieved she wouldn't be the one to say no again. Especially, after Jasper's friends had made that crack about her not wanting to hang out with him the other day.

Phoebe heard Anna's warning in her head again and tried not to feel too upset. She glanced down at her nails; they did look really nice. She made a mental note to pamper herself more, because she deserved it and not because she wanted to impress someone else.

Chapter Eight

It turned out that the Anderson's didn't even end up attending church on Sunday. This was a rare occurrence, but Phoebe's dad was still working on getting the loader out of a pond. Phoebe's mom ended up going with her dad for support, and the rest of the house was pretty quiet. Phoebe felt the tension between Mary and Anna all day. Tabby ended up having a friend over, so Mary took care of them. Anna went out, where Phoebe wasn't sure. So, Phoebe had just spent the entire day in her room either studying, dancing around or laying on her bed watching Netflix on her phone.

After school on Monday, Phoebe was getting ready to head home. She was assigned an essay on her book of choice that she wanted to start to work on and hopefully finish before the weekend. She didn't want to get her hopes up, but she was wishing that Jasper might ask for a rain check on Sunday, she knew her homework would have to be done.

"Hey there, little Anderson," a male voice floated over her as she bent down to pick up the remaining books in her locker, "I was hoping to catch you before you left." Phoebe turned around to see Liam David leaning on the locker next to hers.

"Hey, Liam" Phoebe was a little shocked. Liam and Phoebe had attended school together since kindergarten. They were friendly to each other, but she wouldn't really call him a close friend. Liam was now one of the most popular guys in Hillwood High. He was also the captain of the Hillwood Stallions basketball team and co-captain for the baseball team.

"So, as you know prom is coming up soon," Phoebe's heart stopped. *Was he seriously going to ask me to prom?* She shook her head. There was no way she realized. He would be bringing Brittany or one of the other girls in their clique. "I am most likely being nominated for prom king and I was wondering if I could get your support?" He flashed her a dazzling smile that nearly all the girls at Hillwood High would have swooned over. Phoebe felt like she must be immune to it since they knew each other for so long and had seen him pee his pants back in grade one.

"That depends on who you're up against." Phoebe smirked. She was just teasing him. Things like prom king and queen didn't have any impact on her. She didn't really care who won.

"Oh well, you know probably Neal and Ollie." They were two of Liam's best friends. Actually, they were a group of four that everyone around the school, including themselves, called L.I.O.N – Liam, Ian, Oliver, and Neal. All of them were jocks, all of them were good looking, all of them were sought after. Phoebe didn't really see the infatuation. She continued to shove her books in her bag and smile up at his shaggy brown hair covered face. His blue eyes twinkling back at her.

"Well, since you were first to ask me, you can have my vote." She slammed the locker door and swung her bag onto her shoulder.

"Awesome! This is exactly why you campaign early!" Liam threw his fist up into the air as a celebration. "Thanks, Pheebs, I knew I could count on my longest friend." With that, he turned around and jogged down the hall. Guys put their hands up in the air to high five him as he passed, and the girls batted their eyelashes. Phoebe rolled her eyes and started to walk towards the exit.

"That was so cute. For a second there you thought he was actually going to ask you to prom, didn't you?" Brittany's back was up against her locker a few doors down from Phoebes.

"No, I didn't," Phoebe lied.

"Sure, you did. I saw it in your face. Phoebe we both know that none of the LIONs would ever go with you. You aren't at their level." Brittany smirk and looked at her long fluorescent pink polished nails.

"Whatever you say, Brittany." Phoebe turned and ignored her. She never understood what Brittany's issue with her was, but she chose to turn the other cheek, just like she learned in Sunday school all those years ago.

"That's right, Pheebs," Brittany stressed the ees in her name, "it is whatever I say. Remember that."

When Phoebe got into her car, she slammed the door shut to let out some of her frustration. Better on her car than with words she would love to direct at Brittany. She laid her head back against the car's headrest. Why was everything so complicated lately? She barely saw her friends, there was tension between Mary and Anna, and she could not shake the feeling of unease about the future. What was she doing wrong? She wanted to feel confident in herself and her choices. She was starting to tear up when she heard her phone vibrating in her bag. It was probably Jenn or Maggie wondering where she was and why she didn't meet them when the bell rang. Phoebes eyes grew huge when she realized that it was someone else.

Jasper: Everything is good. Just some team sponsor stuff. Tommy wants to thank you for the bread. He wants to know what this weekend's special is.

Phoebe's heart started to beat a little fast. She had wanted to text Jasper so many times yesterday but held back, nervous that she would become even more smitten, or he would find her annoying.

Phoebe: I am glad everything is okay…

Phoebe tried to think of something else to say. She didn't want to end the conversation there.

Phoebe: I am glad everything is okay. So happy Tommy liked the bread. I am not sure what the special is on Saturday. I get surprised every time I walk in. I do know that when I work tomorrow after school it is Krispy Kreme day!

Phoebe sat in her car for about five minutes just starring at her phone waiting for it to go off again, but nothing happened. She decided to drive home. Jasper must be too busy to text with her. Another sign she thought that he just wanted to be friends.

When Phoebe got home, she went right up to her small room and started working on her paper for English Literature. She decided to write about Pride and Prejudice by Jane Austen. She knew it was probably a bit overdone, but it was one of her favourites and she knew it so well that she didn't have to reread any of it. She worked on it more as a distraction trying to ignore her thoughts about Jasper. Time flew by and Phoebe had gotten the majority of the assigned essay done when her mom called up about dinner. They all sat around the table and Mr. Anderson was in a great mood explaining how they finally pulled the loader out of the pond with barely any damage. Everyone laughed when he told them about how one of the foremen was so hot and frustrated with the whole issue, he started swimming around in the pond to cool off. After dinner, her parents decided they wanted to take in the spring air and go for a walk. Phoebe said she would pass on the offer so she could finish working on her essay. That was one of the only reasons her parents would let her out of a family thing.

It was ten o'clock and Phoebe had finished off her essay. She didn't get any of her other short assignments finished, but she was so happy to have completed her one large project for the week. When the shop wasn't busy at work tomorrow, she knew she could work on her smaller ones. She snuggled into her bed and was about to turn off the light when she saw a flash come from her bedside table.

Jasper: Krispy Kreme! Those are one Tommy's favourites. I am not sure if I should tell him or not. ☺

Phoebe couldn't help but smile. She felt a little giddy. He was texting her again.

Phoebe: What isn't Tommy's favourite? It sounds like he likes everything!

Her heart stopped. She wondered if she would actually get back to her this time or would he be non-responsive. The phone was quiet for a minute. Phoebe felt foolish for letting herself get excited. She put her phone back down on the table. Then the screen lit up again in her darkened room. She hurriedly picked it up almost blinding herself.

Jasper: You're right. He does love everything except strawberries. Not sure what it is about them.

Phoebe let out a giggle. She felt so silly being this giddy, but she couldn't stop herself.

Phoebe: What is your favourite?

Jasper: Sourdough bread. My mom used to make it all the time back home.

Phoebe: Mrs. Barker makes an amazing sourdough. Next time it's on the menu I'll save you a loaf.

She pressed send hoping it didn't sound too pushy or clingy. Then quickly she sent another message hoping that it would distract a little from the one she just sent.

Phoebe: Where is home?

Jasper was silent on the other again for a what felt like forever, but was really not even a minute before she saw the three little typing dots on the screen.

Jasper: Georgia. Yes, please save me like ten loaves. I miss my mom's cooking so much. We get really good meal plans at Fendry, especially athletes, so I shouldn't complain, but I miss home cooking.

Phoebe didn't know what to say next, but she didn't want to end the conversation. She sat there pleading with herself to think of something to say but couldn't come up with anything. Her phone started to buzz again.

Jasper: Do you have a favourite?

Phoebe smiled and started to wiggle into the pillows in her bed, making herself more comfortable.

Phoebe: I know it probably sounds boring, but one of my favourite things from the bakery are chewy oatmeal cookies. No raisins.

Jasper: That doesn't sound boring. That's why they call them classic.

Phoebe: I never thought of it like that, but that's so true.

Phoebe bit her lip nervous that they might have run out of something to talk about again. She had only talked to Jasper a few times before. She wasn't sure how much to ask without seeming like a silly high school girl. Did he, a big baseball college guy even want to continue to talk with her? Anna's words flashed through her mind again. That Jasper was a really nice guy, but he was to everyone. She shouldn't start to think of it as anything more than him being friendly. They had stopped texting for over five minutes. Phoebe felt like such a little schoolgirl rereading their messages over again to herself before she put her phone down. She was nearing the end of their typed conversation when those three little dots popped up on the screen again.

Jasper: So, how was your Monday?

Phoebe could feel her cheeks starting to hurt from smiling at her phone. He was really trying to keep their conversation going. She decided to stop holding back. Just be yourself and go for it. *Be Confident* she thought. She typed out a longer message telling him about how the workload was starting to die down now being in her senior year. She always told him how most of the seniors were just focusing on waiting for their college acceptance letters and prom. Jasper asked what her school was doing for prom and if she was excited to go. Phoebe explained that she was excited and about all the themes that were up for vote on Friday. They tossed around jokes about each one. The conversation was flowing so easily between them.

Jasper: Where did you apply for college?

Phoebe: Dover Christian, UCLA – because one of my best friends begged me to apply with her, and Fendry.

Jasper: Cool. Where do you want to go?

Phoebe: Fendry. I like being close to my family. I know some people don't. It would also be the least expensive, and I know they have a good Education Program.

Jasper: Right. Sorry, I remember you telling me this at church.

Phoebe was shocked. She barely remembered telling him at church about her college hopes. It made her feel a little bit special that he recalled their quick conversation. "Don't let it go to your head, Pheebs," she whispered to herself.

Jasper: Well, I hope you get to go where you want to. Fendry is a pretty cool school, although I am probably biased. I think you would really like I here.

Phoebe: Thanks. I think I would too. I hope I find out soon. I am pretty anxious.

Jasper: Acceptance letters will come sooner than you think. Just enjoy the last few months of your senior year. One piece of advice. Pray about it. I know that can sound cheesy, but it really can help. I felt so lost when trying to choose a college to go to. There was a bunch of offers… Anyways, someone asked me if I had been praying about it. I hadn't, but when I did, God answered. I can't explain how, but He did, and I knew Fendry was where I was supposed to be.

Phoebe nibbled on her pink fingernails she had just painted the day before. She had to admit she hadn't prayed about it at all. She was so consumed lately in trying to be confident in her choices and making decisions on her own, but maybe that was the problem. She was so focus on doing it by herself. She needed to start praying and be confident that God would show her the way.

Jasper: Wow, I really sounded like an old man there… Sorry.

Phoebe: I wouldn't say old… Let's just call it wise. ☺

Jasper: Wise, eh? I'll take it.

Jasper: I have to go. We have an early morning team meeting tomorrow and I didn't realize how late it was.

Phoebe looked at the time on her clock. It was already eleven thirty. How had time passed so fast? She couldn't believe that she had been texting with Jasper for an hour and a half.

Phoebe: Wow, sorry. I didn't realize that time either. Have a good night.

Jasper: Good night, Phoebe.

Phoebe hugged her phone close to her chest. She didn't care if she was acting like a pre-teen girl or not. She couldn't stop herself from feeling giddy.

She had officially developed a huge crush on Jasper Brown and couldn't deny it anymore. Laying her head back on her pillow, she started to pray.

Jesus, please help me to follow you and lean more on you. I know you want what is best for me and I know you have a purpose for my life. Could you please reveal what that is to me Lord? I want to live for you, I want to be confident in my faith and have that be reflected in my choices. Like Anna was saying – it is what I do with the talents you have given me that matters, but Lord, can you show me what my talents are? Amen.

Phoebe felt a little lighter after praying and within minutes she fell asleep with a huge grin on her face.

Chapter Nine

Tuesday came and went. Everyone was running around chatting frantically about which prom theme would be best and who they thought was going to be nominated for prom king and queen. They had a large assembly in the morning just for the juniors and seniors to go over the voting process on both topics. Since the assembly, none of the students had focused on any classes and the teachers just seemed to let it go. The air was filled with pure excitement. Phoebe was excited too, although, she really didn't have any preference about prom. She was just excited to go and spend a last hooray with her besties. They had all made a promise at the beginning of the year that they would go together. Phoebe hoped that they would still like the idea as everyone was swarming around in elation. Promposal ideas were being discussed, which ones were the cutest, which ones the girls would definitely not like. Girls were starting to stand in crowds and giggle as all the guys passed by. Phoebe had no prospects of going with a date. She had some guy friends, but they all had girlfriends already and Phoebe was not really interested in having a fake date. She wanted to go with her besties.

Phoebe climbed into the car quickly after the home bell went off. She was due at work at 3:00. She was already cutting it close, and she didn't want to get stopped again with questions about what theme she would vote for or who she should vote king and queen. She knew Jenn would probably be looking for her. She would have to call and apologize later after work.

Phoebe peeled out of the school parking lot and let out a huge sigh. The assembly made all the seniors feel like the school year was coming to an end; their high school years were coming to an end. Phoebe tried not to think about getting her college acceptance letters or rejection letters in the mail. She knew they could be coming any time in the next few weeks. The waiting was horrible.

Phoebe let out another sigh as she pulled into the parking lot behind the bakery. The five-minute drive from school didn't seem to take the edge off the anxious energy that was buzzing through her. At least, her shift was only three hours today and the first two weren't really busy. It was generally college kids who just wanted to sit on their computers sipping a hot beverage. After five was the rush before closing since everyone would get off work and be heading in to grab some bread or pot pies for dinner that night.

As she walked into the bakery, the scent of sugary dough floated through the air making Phoebe's stomach gurgle. Krispy Kreme day! She hustled into the back to put her things away and hopefully grab a donut to eat before she had to be on the till for the rest of the afternoon. It was as if Mrs. Barker read her mind; there was a donut on a plate beside her employee cubby. She immediately picked it up and took a large, delicious bite. It melted in her mouth, and she moaned at the sticky sugary goodness.

"I see you found the little treat I left you." Mrs. Barker winked at Phoebe. She was wearing her standard pink and white Barker's Bakery apron and as usual it was covered in flour.

"Thank you so much." Phoebe licked the sticky sugar off her lips. "I was so hungry, and the divine smell of the shop made it even worse when I walked in."

"Feed the hungry and help those in trouble. Then your light will shine out from the darkness and the darkness around you will be bright as noon." Mrs. Barker smiled at her. "Isaiah 58:10."

"Well, your light is shining as bright as noon right now." Phoebe smiled. "I was hungry and feeling troubled about it, but you made it better." She giggled as she brushed the crumbs off her shirt, feeling a little embarrassed about how aggressively she ate her donut. Mrs. Baker let out a light laugh and shook her head. She turned around and Phoebe took that as her cue to get up to the front counter. She grabbed her matching apron like the one Mrs. Barker had on and scurried upfront wiping her mouth to make sure it was clear of the gooey sugar.

As it turned out, this Tuesday was the same as every Tuesday. Phoebe was actually able to get the majority of her reading assignments done. Not that she had wanted to, but the shop was so slow, and she got tired of wiping down the glass front where people could look at all of the bakery's goodies. Then a few minutes after five o'clock, cars started to pull into the parking lot in a frenzy. Phoebe braced herself for the after-work rush. Cole, a college student who usually worked in the back on Tuesdays came out front to the counter.

"I thought you would like some help out here. We are finished baking for the day, and I know how the after five rushes can be. Especially, on Krispy Kreme day." Phoebe had never spent a lot of time working with Cole before. The Tuesday shift was the only one that they had together and generally Cole was stuck in the kitchen doing prep work, so they never had time to interact. Today, though, Phoebe was not going to ask any questions of why he didn't have prep and just accepted the help. The line to the counter was now out the door. Cole started grabbing the flat boxes and coaxing them into shape.

They worked beside each other in sync. It was almost as if one could read the other's mind. Phoebe was processing the orders and taking payments, while Cole was filling them as finishing off every sale with his dazzling smile and a "have a wonderful evening". Phoebe never noticed, but Cole was kind of an attractive guy, and he could be really sweet to the customers too. He had a great personality for sales.

Closing was sneaking up quickly and Phoebe was shocked about how much fun she was having. Cole's happy demeanour was contagious. He continuously made her and the customers laugh. Phoebe had excused herself to the washroom when there was a break in customers. With only five minutes to go, she heard the bell on the door chime as she made her way back to the front counter.

"Hey, guys, you just barely made it in time. I was just about to lock the doors. What can I get you?" Cole's voice had change to one of annoyance. Phoebe hustled around the corner to help him out. When she saw who was standing on the other side of the counter, she froze in place.

"Hey, Wally Pheebs!" There was Thomas leaning across the counter near the cash register and standing next to him, Phoebe recognized two other college baseball players she had met briefly before, Parker and Leo. However, it was who was standing behind them that made Phoebe freeze, Jasper. Cole turned around to look at Phoebe. The frown on his face seemed to deepen. He took two steps back from the cash register and motioned his hands towards it, as if to say, they are here for you. Phoebe moved behind the counter.

"Hey, guys. I wasn't expecting to see you here." Phoebe smiled at them all. She was trying to make eye contact with Jasper, but he stayed quiet in the back behind the other three huge baseball players.

"Are you kidding? When I heard today was Krispy Kreme day, I finished our practice sprints faster than anyone else, to make sure we got here in time."

"Maybe, we should put Krispy Kreme's at all the bases, so he'll run to them faster at games." Leo nudged Parker and they both started snickering and gave each other a high five for the clever joke. Thomas just smiled. You could tell he didn't care what the other guys were saying.

"Please, tell me you have some left." Phoebe could practically see Thomas salivating over the thought of the donuts. At first, she thought she might try and trick him, saying they were all out, but the desperate look on his face made her decide not to.

"We do. We only have a few left and since you're the last ones to come into the store, I can give you the end of day sale. Buy one and get one free."

"Phoebe Anderson, you are too good to me," Thomas said, rubbing his hands together in excitement. Phoebe turned around expecting to have Cole there to help her put all the donuts into a box like they had been doing for the past hour, but he was gone. She quickly grabbed some boxes from under the counter and loaded them up with the remaining donuts. A total of 20. Thomas clapped his hand enthusiastically every time she put another donut into the box. Leo and Parker had decided to take their teasing comments to the table nearby and quickly got into a heated discussion about what seemed to be a rival team and their best players. Jasper moved so that he was standing beside Thomas. Phoebe looked up at him and felt herself blush when he made eye contact and smiled.

"Is your family going to church this Sunday?" Jasper asked in his deep rich voice.

"I think so." Phoebe nodded closing the last box of donuts.

"Thomas and I are going to work on his aunt's backyard again. Try to get some more stuff pulled out," Jasper started.

"She is getting pretty annoyed with the mess out back. I can't say I blame her." Thomas pulled out his wallet and put some bills onto the counter.

"Do you think you'd be up for that rain check?" Jasper was looking directly at Phoebe's face. Thomas smiled huge and nodded his head. Looking back and forth between Jasper and Phoebe.

"Um, yeah, that sounds like it would be fun. I'll just pass it by my dad and text you later tonight?" Phoebe handed Thomas his change, which he picked up and put directly into the tip jar beside the cash register. He gave Phoebe a wink.

"Well, now that all of that is handled, we really need to get back to the dorms before coach has a fit." Thomas turned to Phoebe. "We have a game next week against our biggest rivals, which means coach has been riding our tails. You should come out and watch!" He looked so excited at his revelation to invite Phoebe to come watch their game, she had to let out a giggle. Thomas was one of the happiest and nicest people Phoebe had ever met.

"I would really like that." Phoebe looked at Jasper. He was now looking at his phone in his hand and texting furiously back. Phoebe wished he seemed as happy about the potential of her coming to watch their game as Thomas was.

"Well, thanks again, Pheebs, for these donuts." All of the baseball boys moved towards the door. A chorus of "see yas" and "thanks, Phoebes" rang through the air. As fast as they had appeared, they had vanished. Phoebe was beaming as the door closed, but then felt a little sad that Jasper had been so distracted. She wished she could have talked to him more.

"I wouldn't get too attached to any of those guys." Cole's voice made Phoebe jump. She had thought he had left already.

"Cole, you scared me. I thought you went home." Phoebe moved towards the front door to lock it and turn off the lights.

"I wouldn't leave you here by yourself with them." Cole started to close the cash register and turned off the lights in the display cabinet.

"What do you mean?" Phoebe continued her routine of closing the bakery.

"Those guys have quite the reputation on campus. They go through girls like they go through water, Phoebe. Be careful. They work hard to get you to adore them and then they drop you." Phoebe couldn't believe what Cole was saying.

"You know you are talking about Thomas, right? He is practically the nicest person I have ever met."

"Sugar gets all the flies and bees get all the honey, but flies bite and bees sting." Cole shrugged and walked out back to the kitchen. Phoebe followed behind him, reluctantly. She didn't want to believe what he was saying.

"It appears that I have upset you. I am sorry for that, Pheebs." Cole stressed her nickname that the baseball boys had used. "It's true. I have seen it happen many times before. I just don't want you to fall into that trap too. You're one of the good ones." He winked at her. Phoebe felt more and more uncomfortable. They had just spent a crazy fun filled hour together working in sync, but the feeling of friendship they had just built started to dissipate. Was it just because Cole had said something that Phoebe did not want to hear or was it something more that was making these feeling appear? She wasn't sure.

"Thanks for looking out for me, I guess." Phoebe grabbed her belongings and followed Cole out to the parking lot where both their cars were waiting.

"I've got your back, Phoebe." He smiled. "I hope we get to work another shift together soon. It was fun. The time went by so fast." Phoebe nodded her head in reply and climbed into her car. She decided that she would take Cole's advice with caution. She didn't know him well at all, but then again, she didn't really know Thomas or Jasper either. However, Thomas and Jasper had never made her feel used before. She would be careful, but she still wanted to be friends with them, and secretly, maybe, more than friends with Jasper. Phoebe turned on her car and built up her courage again, hoping that this time she could ask her dad about Sunday.

Chapter Ten

When Phoebe got home from work, her dad was busy at the kitchen table. There were papers everywhere and he had a frown on his face. The "think" crease line on his forehead seemed to be even bigger than usual, so she knew now was not the time to ask him about Sunday. Phoebe washed up for dinner like her mom told her to and then went upstairs to her bedroom to do some reading. Except, her mind could not focus on her biology book. She finally decided to close it and go take a shower, when she realized she read the same sentence over at least five times and hadn't retained any of the information. All she could think about was how Jasper seemed really distant today. Thomas was always so happy and paid more attention to her than Jasper did. Jasper never really talked to her when other people, except for Thomas, were around. Maybe, she did need to take Cole's advice. Her head was swimming. She realized that she was probably over analyzing everything, but she couldn't stop herself.

After Phoebe showered, she could hear her sisters arguing about something downstairs. Things between her older sisters weren't settling and grew more tense. She wasn't sure what was going on between them, but she knew that she did not have the energy or mental capacity to deal with it currently. Dinner was quiet after Mr. Anderson stated he didn't want to hear anymore arguing or nonsense. All four girls helped their mom clean up after and went their separate ways. Phoebe decided to climb into her bed at 9:00 and called it a night. Reflecting on her day, she felt a call to pray.

Lord, I have so many questions going through my mind. I know you are always there for me, and I just ask for your guidance in my life. I need help with my relationships with others Jesus. Please, help me to continue to form connections with those who you want me to but help me also to know when I need to let go. Please, also help me to know which university I need to go to, help me to make the right choices for my future. I want to please you Lord and live a life that is based on you and reflects you in all my actions. Please, help me to be confident. Amen.

It was officially Friday. Prom themes vote day. When Phoebe got to school there was electricity from all the excitement in the air. There was an announcement in the morning stating that all votes for the theme must be completed by end of lunch period, as well as all nominations for prom king and queen. Anna was right. Now that March was over and they were well into April, the teachers seemed to put a break on the workload for the seniors. It was probably because "prom brain" seemed to become a real thing. No one could pay attention for long. Maggie, Jenn and Phoebe finally got to eat lunch together in what felt like forever.

"I am so thankful we can officially get this theme picked! I have both my fabrics for each theme picked out to make my dress. I want to go to the store at the end of school to pick it up and start working on it. Mrs. Myers said I could use it for my end of year project as well. How awesome is that?" Jenn was buzzing like a bee filled with jubilation.

"That's awesome," Phoebe said filling her mouth with the ham and cheese sandwich she made earlier this morning. "I can't wait to see what you come up with."

"No wonder you won't have a date to prom, Phoebe. No one wants to sit with you when you eat like that." Brittany and her friends snickered as they passed by Phoebe's table to the back corner table all the jocks and cheerleaders sat at. It was considered the "cool kid table". Phoebe had once said that term to Anna last year. Anna, who sat at that very table almost every year she attended high school, denied it, and said all were welcome. Phoebe knew that Anna probably felt that way, but to anyone else who didn't normally sit there felt like an outcast. She had heard a number or freshmen saying, "when we sit at the cool table," or "when I make the cheer team next year, I am going to sit at the back table". She had to admit that more than once she wished she would be welcome there, but as the years went by, she wanted to avoid the company there, specifically Brittney.

"Don't listen to her, Pheebs. She seems to be power tripping today because she knows she will be in the running for prom queen. You'd think that would make her nicer, but it seems to be having the opposite effect." Maggie glared at Brittney and her friends as they greeted the LIONS at "their table". "You know, I think that someone should knock her off her high horse." Maggie still hadn't taken her eyes off them. She suddenly stood up and took her lunch tray, emptying the remaining food into the garbage can and headed out of the cafeteria.

"What just happened?" Jenn looked at Phoebe in disbelief.

"No idea." Phoebe was genuinely confused. "Let's just clean up our stuff and go cast our votes."

"Sounds good!" Jenn practically bounced her whole way to the voting station. A lot of other people had the same idea in mind causing a large line up. Mr. Xu and another teacher Phoebe recognized as a grade nine science teacher were manning the voting table. They didn't want any students in charge, so that no one could say the votes were tampered with. That happened a few years ago and cause a huge rift in the student body. Finally, the girls were able to cast their votes right before the bell rang. They both voted for masquerade.

"I can't meet up at your locker later. I have a meeting for a group project. But I will call you this weekend and we can plan the details for our girl's night." Jenn waved as she made her way through the hall. The rest of the day was the same as the morning. Little was happening in the classes so Phoebe was able to finish all the reading and homework she would have had for the weekend. Having all her homework done would be a positive, if she wanted to go out for lunch with Jasper and Tommy after church. She really needed to ask her dad about going. She convinced herself that she would do it tonight. Jasper hadn't texted her since their meeting at the Bakery earlier that week. She hoped he hadn't given up on the idea yet.

"The votes are in!" said a voice over the PA system at the very end of last period. A hush went over the entire classroom. "The theme for this year's prom is MASQUERADE!" There were hoots and hollers heard from down the hall mixed in was a much lower volume of boos. "We also have the official nominations for prom king and queen." Everyone stopped their cheering quickly. Phoebe really didn't care all that much about any of this, but the excitement was palpable, so she sat on the edge of her seat. "Prom King nominations are Liam Davis, Neal Yang, and Oliver Miller!" Neal and Oliver were both in Phoebe's class. They jumped up, high-fived each other and started to take bows and the rest of the class applauded them. Neal's girlfriend Laura Garci (also Brittney's best friend) was swooning over him and giggling with delight. "And the nominations for prom queen are…" The boys sat down and Phoebe watch Laura grab Neal's hand for support. "Brittany Mae, Laura Garci." Laura jumped up and gave Neal a kiss on the lips. Phoebe couldn't help but laugh. Even though Laura was best friends with Brittany, and they were not friends, she was excited for her. *What would it be like to be nominated and with your boyfriend? It must be pretty exciting.* Phoebe decided she would vote for them both. "… and … Maggie Ganbold!" Phoebe's head snapped towards the PA system along with the 30 other students in the classroom.

"What?" screeched Laura. "Maggie? It should have been Charlotte." She immediately pulled out her phone and started texting. Phoebe wanted to do the same and ask Maggie if she knew anything about the nomination, but the bell rang, and everyone started packing up. She waited for Maggie by her locked at the end of the day, but she never showed. Brittany, Laura were consoling a crying Charlotte a few lockers down. Phoebe did not want to be in their firing range of emotions, so she left for home. She tried texting Jenn and Maggie in their group message, but neither of them had replied. Dinner turned out to be later than usual since Mr. Anderson was trying to finish up a job. He was telling his wife how difficult it was to find people to work this summer and was thinking about posting job information on the Fendry job page for college students. Phoebe took the mention of Fendry College students as a sign to ask her dad about Sunday lunch.

"Hey, Dad?" Phoebe started as she was clearing the dishes from the table. Mr. Anderson turned to look at his daughter. *Now or never,* Phoebe thought.

"A friend asked if Mary, Anna, and I could go to lunch after church with him and his friend. He actually said that Tabby could even come too, if she wanted."

"Wanted to go to lunch with who?" Tabby popped her head up from the couch in the living room right across from the kitchen. Phoebe didn't even know she was there.

"Jasper and Tommy. You met them a few weeks ago at church, remember?"

"Oh, yeah, that sounds like it would be so much fun. Can we go, Daddy? Tommy is a total babe!" Phoebe and Mr. Anderson's mouths both dropped. Phoebe could not believe her sister had said that. She would never in her life tell her father a guy was a "total babe." She wasn't sure it was going to help with them being allowed to go either.

"Do I know Jasper or Tommy?" Mr. Anderson asked trying to focus back on Phoebe, but she could tell he was still taken back by his youngest's comments.

"Tommy is Alice Hernandez's nephew. Remember how she was telling us about how her nephew and friend had agreed to help clean her backyard?" Phoebe was shocked that her mother had stepped into the conversation. She usually always sat back in these situations.

"Oh, yes. I was actually quite shocked that two boys agreed to take that mess on. I told her I give her a fair price to help out. I know it's been tough since Freddy passed. But she didn't want to wait. She said she couldn't stand looking at it any longer, not that I can blame her." Phoebe was happy her dad knew of the boys, but was getting really anxious waiting for him to answer.

"Can we go, Daddy?" Tabby broke the silence. Phoebe wanted to kiss her outspoken sister for getting the conversation back on topic. She really wanted to go and had never asked her dad anything to do with boys before, she didn't know what to expect.

"Well, why don't you introduce them to me at church and then we will go from there." Her father turned away, signalling the end of the conversation. It wasn't a yes, but it also wasn't a no. So, Phoebe decided not to push it and would take that answer. After finishing the clean-up and helping her mom fold some laundry, Phoebe headed upstairs to get ready for bed because tomorrow she had another early Saturday morning shift. Anna had said Phoebe could have the car tomorrow morning, since it was supposed to rain, as long as she could have it the afternoon to go shopping with Brittany and friends for prom dresses. Phoebe bit her tongue and refrained from telling Anna about her run-ins with Brittney that week. She didn't want to cause anymore friction in the house. She knew Anna had a soft spot of Brittney for some reason. Anna said she would also pick up the green dress for Phoebe while she was at the mall.

Laying down in bed she looked at her phone. Still nothing from Jenn or Maggie but there was a message from a number that Phoebe didn't know.

Unknown: Wally Pheebs!

Phoebe smiled. It had to be Tommy; he was the only one that called her that.

Tommy: Make sure you text me tomorrow's special. We just won our game tonight against the Tornados! I need some celebratory baked goods.

Of course, Tommy would want to celebrate with food. Phoebe may have not known him long, but she did know that boy loved food. It made her laugh.

Phoebe: I am assuming this is Tommy. Congratulations on your win! I will text you early tomorrow to let you know.

Tommy: Sorry, I should have led with that. Let me start again.

Tommy: Hey! It's Tommy. Jasper gave me your number; I hope that's okay. I need some amazing Wally baked goods to celebrate our win.

Phoebe: Ha-ha! Yes, that's okay.

Phoebe secretly wished that Jasper would have texted her, but she was happy to talk with Tommy as well.

Tommy: Great! We are driving to my aunt's tomorrow. Are you ladies up for lunch on Sunday?

Phoebe bit her nails. Would it sound childish that her dad wanted to meet them before they were allowed to go? This was Tommy, he never once made her feel bad before. She should just be honest.

Phoebe: I asked my dad, tonight. He said he would like to meet you guys first. Is that okay?

Phoebe waited for his response. She started getting nervous, when he didn't text her back right away. Maybe, she was wrong. Maybe, he did think she was an overprotected baby.

Tommy: Sure! Makes sense. I am great with parents; I can't say the same for Jasper, though! HA-HA. Got to go, Wally. We are celebrating tonight. Text me about those baked yummies!

Phoebe: I will!

Phoebe was relieved and excited. She would let her sisters know about the lunch plans tomorrow. She was sure Anna and Tabby would be fine with it, but not so sure about Mary. Would that be a deal breaker for her dad?

Work the next morning was the same as usual. Phoebe had texted Tommy to let him know the special was lemon squares, but hadn't received a reply by the time she was ready to leave. She decided to pick up a dozen. Six to treat her family for dessert tonight and the other six was for Tommy. Hopefully, he liked lemon. Phoebe remembered that Jasper said he loved everything but strawberries. When she tried to pay for the squares, Mrs. Baker told her just to take them. They were a thank you for being a dedicated early Saturday morning employee.

Chapter Eleven

The squares were a hit after dinner and Phoebe made sure the remaining six were put in the fridge for safekeeping. She hadn't heard anything from Tommy or Jasper, for that matter. Mary and Anna were on clean up duty, but Phoebe decided to pitch in. She wanted to hear about Anna's shopping trip with Brittany. She had found her dress bag on her bed before dinner.

"Laura ended up getting this beautiful bright purple dress. It has this gorgeous low back and deep v in the front. It must have been new because it definitely wasn't there when we went." That was okay with Phoebe. From the description she didn't like it more than her green dress and she was pretty sure a deep v was something that her parents would not consider appropriate for a "young woman of God". That was fine, she was sure she wouldn't have the confidence to pull it off either. "Get this! Charlotte actually ended up getting that pink dress that Tabby loved!"

"Really?" Mary asked the shock and her face matched what Phoebe was feeling.

"Really, but it actually looked good on her. Nothing against you Pheebs," Anna smiled. "You and Charlotte have very different body types and that dress also really suits her personality."

"None taken," and that was the truth. Phoebe knew that her long lanky body and quiet demeanour were defiantly different from Charlotte's curves and extremely bubbly personality. It was a dress perfect for a vice captain cheerleader.

"She was really upset about not getting nominated for prom queen. Did you have any idea about Maggie?"

"No, I was so shocked! I messaged her a number of times but didn't hear anything back. I was going to call her tomorrow after church," Phoebe said.

"Wow, good for Maggie. I am super proud of her for going after prom queen. Being class president and voted prom queen would look amazing to colleges," Mary stated as she loaded the dishwasher.

Of course, that would be what Mary thought of. Phoebe giggled to herself.

"Brittany didn't find a dress, though. She said she wanted something that really made a statement. She might go out of town to look." Anna shrugged. Phoebe was curious to see what Brittany would end up picking. It would probably be something really flashy and revealing. Phoebe kept those thoughts to herself. She knew she would be scolded for speaking ill of someone by her sisters. They would give her the speech about trying to show Brittany God's love again. It's not that Phoebe didn't agree with it, but it was really hard to do with someone who always made fun of you and tried to get under your skin.

"So," Phoebe began to change the topic, "Dad said we could possibly go out for lunch with Jasper and Tommy tomorrow after church, but he wants to meet them first." Both Anna and Mary stopped what they were doing and turned to face Phoebe.

"Really?" Anna began to say in a teasing voice, but Mary cut her off.

"Sorry, Pheebs, but I don't think I can tomorrow. Andrew and I were going to go out for lunch to celebrate him doing well on his finals." Phoebe cringed, she hoped that wouldn't change her dad's mind. "You should have mentioned it sooner." Phoebe nodded her head. It was true she should have, but it took her so long to get the courage to talk with her parents about it.

"I am good to go." Anna smiled. "I know you have been wanting to have lunch with Jasper forever." Phoebe opened her mouth to protest but Anna held up her hand. "Don't even bother denying it. You have a massive crush on him; I can see it in your eyes every time you say his name. I will help you with getting dad to let us go."

"Thanks Anna." Phoebe sheepishly smiled. There was no point hiding it anymore.

"Just be careful with your heart, Pheebs. Jasper Brown is very well-known, and a lot of girls would love to be seen on his arm. I just don't want you to get hurt."

Mary's caution stuck with Phoebe for the rest of the night. It wasn't the first time she was made aware of Jasper's popularity. She was right. So many girls would want to catch Jasper's attention. She knew she couldn't even compare to the majority of them. She was only a silly high school girl whose dad had to meet him before they could even have lunch together. Phoebe had heard from Anna before about girls running after athletes. The things they would do to get attention from the players was shocking. She was sure girls would go to even greater lengths to get the attention from THEE Jasper Brown, as Jenn called him. Why would she even be on his radar. That's probably why she hadn't heard from him all week. She decided right then she would put her Jasper thoughts into a friend box and not let them wander out again. She needed to be focusing on things like university and her purpose. Seeking comfort, she decided to bring her thoughts to God.

Jesus, I have been talking to you over and over again about the same things. I can't seem to shake Jasper out of my mind, and I am not sure why. I feel self-conscious. Why would he even be interested in someone like me? Can you please help me to move my focus to you Lord. I need to focus on you and what you have planned for me. Please, show me the way. Please, help me to hear from the universities I applied to and decide. I want to start moving on with my life. Oh, and Father, if you could help me fix my thoughts towards Brittney. I know I should try to be kinder, but she just makes it so hard! Amen.

It had been a while since Phoebe found herself praying this consistently and really trying to focus on God. She felt more aware of His presence and was happy, but then she remembered who had reminded her to start praying and seeking God's will. It was Jasper and now he was back in her mind again.

Chapter Twelve

When Phoebe woke up on Sunday morning, she was a ball of nerves. She wanted the meeting to go well between the boys and her dad. She wanted lunch to be fun for everyone, but most of all wanted to be able to keep her head and heart in check with Jasper. Although she put Jasper in the "friend zone" along with Tommy, she still wanted to look nice. She pulled out a cute white tea length skirt. It had tiny cute cherries on it and paired it with a long sleeve red fitted shirt. With it now being mid-April, spring was in the air and Phoebe felt like the outfit complimented that. She pulled her hair up into a cute high ponytail. She felt fresh and ready to take on the day.

"Wow, Pheebs, you look really nice," Mary said as she and Anna joined Phoebe downstairs for breakfast.

"Thanks." Phoebe smiled and smoothed out her skirt. She felt cute and confident.

"You can wear my white flats today, if you want. I think they would go really well with that outfit," Anna suggested.

"Okay, thanks, Anna." Mr. and Mrs. Anderson joined their three eldest girls in the kitchen for a quick breakfast.

"Where is Tabby?" Mr. Anderson asked look at the rest of his girls. Everyone shook their head. It was strange that Tabby hadn't made an appearance yet. She was usually one of the first ones down at breakfast. She always wanted to get the good cereal before it was gone. It often left Phoebe with shredded wheat or plain toast.

"Good morning," Tabby sashayed into the kitchen. She was wearing a floral dress with platform sandals and her hair up in a high ponytail like Phoebe. When Tabby turned to face Phoebe, she noticed that she had layers and layers of glossy lip balm on. It wasn't technically lipstick like Mr. Anderson told her she couldn't wear but still made her lips pop. Typical Tabby finding a way to bend the rules to her liking and still get away with it.

"Good morning, sweetie. It looks like more than one of my daughters has really tried to make themselves presentable for the Lord today. At least, I hope that is the reason for all the effort this morning." Mrs. Anderson gave a wink to Phoebe that no one else could see. Phoebe felt her cheeks flush.

"I look nice everyday, Mom. So, I know I can't be the one you are talking about," Tabby stated with a hair flip. "Where is all the good cereal?" She shifted the items in the cupboard around looking for a sugary box of Lucky Charms.

"Sorry, sweetie, you will have to make toast to eat in the van because we are going to be late."

"But, Mom, the crumbs are going to get all in my lip gloss, I don't want toast!" Tabby moaned. Mrs. Anderson shooed Tabby towards the toaster and told the rest of the girls to meet their father as he was already waiting for them in the van again.

The ride to church was quiet except for Tabby telling their mom about how a girl in her class had gotten bangs and how Tabby was thinking she might like to get them too. Phoebe was surprised at how much Tabby was into fashion. Phoebe didn't remember caring or even thinking about hair or lip gloss when she was ten. Tabby continued talking about it all the way into church then quickly said good-bye when they got inside. Mrs. Anderson headed to the kitchen, as always, to see if anyone needed help and Mr. Anderson was going to be an usher. That left Phoebe, Anna, Mary, and Andrew who met them at the front door to find a seat. They decided to sit closer to the back today since many of the rows were filling up near the front. Phoebe slid in the pew, sandwiched between her two sisters. The piano began to play signalling that the service would begin soon.

"Hey, everyone, mind if we sit with you?" Tommy was beaming down at them with Jasper close behind. They both had on black jeans. Tommy was wearing a red button up shirt the same colour as Phoebe's shirt and Jasper had on a green sweater. Phoebe tried to ignore the fact that it made his eyes stand out even more.

"Sure can," Andrew said as he shuffled down the pew so that the boys could both fit in next to him. Pastor Moore walked up the front to welcome everyone and the service began. Phoebe enjoyed the message and really tried to focus on what was being taught. Very fittingly, the message was about seeking guidance from the bible when making decisions in life. Phoebe listened intently on what he was saying, feeling like this message was specifically for her. The major points he brought to light was having trust in God, asking for wisdom and discernment, having a community of believers helping you, using scripture for advice, and to pray about everything. Phoebe made notes in the margin of her bible of points she wanted to remember. She specifically underlined Philippians 4:6 "Do not be anxious about anything, but in everything by prayer and supplication with thanksgiving let your requests be made known to God." Pastor Moore was an amazing speaker. He gave a lot of analogies, which Phoebe really enjoyed. At the end of the service, they stood and headed outside to the front of the church where Andrew had started a conversation with Tommy and Jasper about the Outdoor Plus store going up in Fendry. Phoebe hadn't even heard about it and just stood quietly next to Mary feeling awkward. She was hoping that they still wanted to go out for lunch but didn't want to be pushy and hunt down her parents so that they could meet the boys. Luckily, she saw her mom walk out the front with Tabby and her dad following closely behind them.

"Hi, Tommy!" Tabby ran right up to Tommy and gave him a big hug. Everyone was shocked, including Tommy who froze for a second then patted her back.

"Hey, Tabby, how's it going?" Tommy laughed.

"Oh great. Have you met my parents yet? This is my mom, Ruth, and my dad, John." Again, Tabby full of surprises was totally high-jacking Phoebe's introduction. She wasn't sure if she was happy that she didn't have to do it or mad at her little sister for making her feel invisible. Tommy stuck out his hand to shake Phoebe's dad's hand and then her mom's.

"Mr. and Mrs. Anderson, it is lovely to meet you. I'm Thomas and this is my best friend, Jasper." Jasper reached over to shake Phoebe's parents' hands as well.

"Nice to meet you both," Mr. Anderson said. "I heard you two were undertaking Alice's backyard. That's quite the feat I must admit."

"It is." Tommy nodded his head. "We are getting pretty close to having the whole yard torn up but there is this one tree in the middle that is giving us trouble. The roots go way deeper and further than we thought."

"I know just the one you are taking about." Mr. Anderson laughed. "I told Freddy not to plant that tree there, but he was convinced it would be a great spot."

"That sounds like my uncle." Tommy laughed. "Any suggestion on how to get it out without breaking our backs. I don't think coach with be heartbroken if I didn't play, but I know he would be fuming if Jasper hurt himself over a tree." Tommy patted Jasper's back.

"That's not true," Jasper finally spoke up, "he would be livid if you weren't out on that field, and so would I." He shook his head.

"Well, I do have some ideas. How about you boys come over for lunch and we can figure somethings out." *What?* Phoebe looked at her dad in shock. She couldn't believe her dad was taking over what was and invitation to her for lunch with Jasper and Tommy. First, Tabby trying to take over and now her dad! Phoebe looked at her mom for help.

"Now, John, I think the kids wanted to go out for lunch, remember." Her mom seemed to catch the meaning of Phoebe's stare.

"Oh right, well you all can do that or Ruth and I can throw together a BBQ. I also know there might be some lemon bars in the fridge Phoebe got for you, Tommy. She slapped my fingers when I tried to grab a second one last night." Her dad winked at her. Phoebe's mouth dropped open. Why was her dad doing this to her?

"A barbeque sounds amazing, right Jasper?" Tommy asked his friend.

"It has been a while since we have eaten a home cooked meal." Jasper nodded in agreement. Now Phoebe felt bad. She remembered that one of the things Jasper said he missed most about home was having a home cooked meal. A barbeque at her house wouldn't be horrible and she realized that Tommy and Jasper would probably really appreciate it. Pizza must be a common meal for them.

"Alright, let's head home then. You boys just follow us." Mr. Anderson smiled and headed towards the van. Phoebe could not understand what just happened. She hadn't even spoken a word to either Tommy or Jasper today. Anna grabbed her hand and gave it a squeeze. They smiled at each other, and Anna mouthed "are you okay?" Phoebe nodded. It wasn't how she had pictured today going but she was happy her dad was getting along with both boys so far. She was glad she promised herself they were all just friends. She kept saying that over and over again until they pulled into their driveway. Andrew and Mary pulled in beside the van and Jasper pulled his truck in behind them.

"Come on, Tommy and Jasper, I'll get you both a drink," Tabby said running to the front door. Anna looked at Phoebe and rolled her eyes. This was how the rest of the day would go; Phoebe was sure of it.

"Mary and Andrew, why don't you two go start the grill and put the cushions on the chairs." They had decided to forgo their celebratory lunch with a strong nudge from Mr. Anderson, to join in on the family meal. Tabby led the boys to the table and then grabbed them each a cup of juice.

"Tabby could I also have cup, please?" Phoebe's dad asked as he sat down across from the boys and started up conversation about Mrs. Hernandez's backyard tree issues again. Phoebe moved into the kitchen and started to help her mom pull out all the necessary ingredients for Caesar salad, sausages, potato salad and corn on the cob.

"Good thing I did groceries yesterday." Mrs. Anderson laughed. "Sorry, Phoebe, I know this is probably not what you had in mind when you asked to have lunch with Jasper and Tommy today."

"It's okay, Mom." Phoebe shrugged. It was okay, she decided. They were all just friends. Just friends. *Friends should be able to join her family for a meal. Maggie and Jenn did,* she thought. Anna gathered the plates and took the meat outside for Andrew to start to grill. Phoebe worked side by side with her mom preparing the rest of the food. She would glance up every now and then to watch her dad and the boys deep in conversation about landscaping, then baseball, and then it moved to fishing. Phoebe had no doubt that her father was loving it. Tabby just sat at the table starring at Tommy, laughing loudly at everything he said. Even when it wasn't a joke.

"She appears to be thoroughly enjoying their company. Do you have some competition, Phoebe?" Mrs. Anderson laughed and nudged her.

"Ha-ha, no, we are all just friends." Phoebe shook her head. The more she said it the more it made her accept it.

"Well, they seem to be very nice young men and your dad appears to like them." Mom smiled and put the salads on a tray to carry. "Why don't you go tell them to come outside for lunch."

"Okay." Phoebe shyly approach the dining table. "I think we are all set for lunch," she interrupted her dad telling the story about catching a twenty-pound perch. He was using his hands to how big it was. Phoebe knew he loved to tell that story.

"Great! Thanks, Pheebs, all this talking about fish has really grown my appetite." Mr. Anderson stood, and they all followed. When Phoebe got outside the only spot left at the table was one next to her mom at the very end. Phoebe listened to Anna tell her mom about all the new updos she was learning currently and how her practical exams were going to be held. Mary and Andrew were talking about their dinner plans tonight, where they would celebrate his finals so they could join the family for lunch. At the end of the table, Tabby was talking to Tommy about something very animatedly; Phoebe couldn't make out what it was, but Tabby had him and stitches. That left Jasper and her dad who seemed to be deep in conversation about something. Phoebe was shocked. Both men seemed to be enjoying each other's company greatly.

When everyone was finished, Phoebe stood up with the rest of the Anderson girls while the men stayed at the table and conversed. Phoebe started to load the dishwasher and then filled the sink with water and soap to wash all the remaining dishes that wouldn't fit.

"You cooked; I think that means I should clean." Jaspers came up beside her and grabbed a dish cloth.

"You don't have to do that." Phoebe smiled at him. "You're the guest."

"My mom always said that a polite guest helps out. Plus, I like doing dishes. I kind of find it relaxing." Jasper smiled his crooked grin at her and plunged his hand into the hot water.

"I'll dry," Phoebe said. They worked in silence, and it didn't feel awkward at all to Phoebe.

"Thanks for having us over today for lunch. It really has been a while since either of us had a home cooked meal," Jasper stated as he put more cups into the drying rack.

"No problem. I know my dad really enjoyed having you. I think he likes having more males around the house. He didn't have to talk about hair or nails for once." Phoebe grinned up at Jasper. His height always took her back. She was tall herself, but he made her feel so tiny next to him. "Congratulations on your game by the way; Tommy told me you guys won."

"Yeah, thanks, it was rough but we got it." Jasper calmly finished up the last dish. "We could let the rest dry if that's okay and go sit outside?"

"Sure," Phoebe said. *Just friends,* she thought as she placed her towel on the oven bar to dry. She followed Jasper outside to the swing bench her dad built when they were kids. Everyone else was scattered around the backyard. Tommy was still being entertained by Tabby. Anna was talking with their dad. Mary, Andrew, and her mom had moved some chairs into the sun.

"So did you find out the theme for your prom yet?" Jasper asked as he began to push the swing back and forth with his legs.

"It's masquerade." Phoebe smiled at him. She was shocked that he remembered them talking about that.

"Is that what you wanted?"

"To be honest, I really didn't care; but I did vote for that one." Phoebe shrugged.

"Are you not excited?" Jasper asked.

"Not as much as others. I am excited to spend time and dance with my friends but dressing up and stuff really isn't something I get excited about." There was a long pause as they both watched Tabby and Tommy now playing catch with a baseball. "What was your prom theme?" Phoebe asked trying to break the silence.

"I think it was under the sea." Jasper made a scrunchy face as he tried to remember. "I didn't actually go. I missed it to come sign with Fendry."

"Oh, I'm sorry."

"It's all good. I am not a great dancer anyways. Signing with Fendry was more important."

"My friend Jenn says you are one of the best players in the NCAA." Phoebe cringed. *Why did she say that? Now he would know she was talking about him to her friends. He was always probably so bored of being fawned over.*

"I don't know about that, but I am honoured she thinks so." Jasper smiled at Phoebe.

"Jenn is a massive sports fan. I don't really know that much about baseball, to be honest." *Ugh, just keep digging a hole.* Phoebe thought to herself. *Wait, what does it matter, they were just friends. Right?* She tried to convince herself.

"That's okay. I don't really know much about teaching." Jasper kept the bench swinging. Phoebe was enjoying watching her family all around the backyard. This afternoon was turning out the be way better than pizza would have been.

"Is baseball what you want to do? I mean, do you want to play in the MLB?" Phoebe asked.

"I thought you didn't know anything about baseball?" Jasper smirked at her and gave her side a nudge.

"Okay, I guess I know somethings." Phoebe laughed.

"To be honest, I don't know anymore." Jasper looked like he was lost deep in thought. Phoebe kept quiet for a few minutes and started to feel the mood shifting. She didn't want to upset him. "I really liked what Pastor Moore was preaching about today." Phoebe nodded her head in agreeance. "Major decisions in life really need to be made with focus on the Lord. We need to trust

God and not try to figure it out all by ourselves. Proverbs 3:5 is one of my favourite verses. I also really liked that one in Philippians her mentioned."

"Me, too!" Phoebe exclaimed. "4:6. I underlined it in my bible." Jasper gave her a lopsided smile.

"I know that sometimes I can try to run ahead of God. Like when I really want something to happen. I try to do things to make what I want to occur or to quicken it." Phoebe nodded showing that she knew what he meant. She felt like she had been trying to rush into finding what to do with her life after high school. She now realized she was trying to push her wants ahead of what God was trying to show her. Jasper continued on with his thought, "I know I can also get nervous when choices come up that I have to make but I need to remember not being anxious; God's got it under control. I just need to keep communicating with him." Phoebe had never talked like this about the bible or God with anyone before. It felt so natural and open. Usually, she would clam up and keep her thoughts to herself, but with Jasper she felt like she would never be judged. She valued his insight and hoped that she could have the same kind of relationship with Jesus as he did. They both continued to swing silently on the bench. Jasper seemed to be consumed in his thoughts.

"Um, do you think we should go save Tommy?" Phoebe pointed to Tommy who was now running drills with Tabby.

"Nah, he is loving this probably as much as Tabby. He has a bunch of siblings at home, and I know he is missing them." Tommy pulled his phone out of his pocket and looked up at Jasper.

"Hey, man, Aunt Alice just texted. We should probably head back."

"Sure." Jasper stopped the swing from rocking with a quick stomp of his feet. Phoebe didn't realize how soothing the feeling of rocking next to Jasper was until it ended. Everyone walked the guys to the front door to say good-bye. Phoebe's dad reached out to shake both Tommy and Jasper's hand.

"If you boys decide you want some help with that tree next weekend let me know by Friday morning and we can have a machine shipped there for Saturday."

"Thanks so much, Mr. Anderson. We will let you know before Friday for sure," Jasper said. Both men shook his hand, waved good-bye to the rest of the family and walked out the door towards the car.

"Well, that was a lovely afternoon," Mrs. Anderson said as everyone departed in their own directions. Phoebe had to agree. At first, she was really disappointed that she had to share the company of Tommy and Jasper with her family, but she loved how they got along with everyone. Maybe, now that her dad knew them and he clearly liked them if he offered to help with his machines, she could hang out with them outside of the family. She did also get some one-on-one time with Jasper. She loved how honest he was with her, and how he challenged her to think in different ways, especially with her faith. Everyone kept telling her to be cautious and not get too attached. She thought back about Cole and how he said he was a womanizer. That was definitely not the Jasper she had sat with on the swing today. She really enjoyed his company.

Even if he isn't interested in me as more than a friend, I want to be satisfied with just having a friendship with him. I feel like I am getting to know the real Jasper, maybe not the one everyone sees in the newspapers or on a baseball field, but his heart, she thought. *Maybe, I am also starting to discover more about my heart as well.*

Chapter Thirteen

It was Friday and Phoebe felt like she could finally take a breath as she walked to pick up her books to bring home for the weekend. She had been called to pick up an extra shift at work for a sick co-worker twice and had worked her normal shifts. The excitement about Prom, college acceptance letters and the nearing end of the school year continued to take over. So, the teachers often let their students use their classes to finish up projects or start review for exams. Phoebe hadn't been able to see much of her friends with everything going on. She did get a brief moment to ask Maggie about her prom queen nomination. Their school had a policy that if the student president wanted to be a part of the prom court, they had an automatic nomination as prom queen. Maggie said she wanted to run so she was given a place. That was where she ran off to at lunch last week.

Maggie had been busy with not only student president duties but now also prom court duties so neither Jenn nor Phoebe had seen very much of her. Jenn would jokingly stop at one of Maggie's prom queen posters and have a conversation with it in place of the real Maggie. Jenn had also been busy with making her prom dress, which was also her final project one of her classes. Phoebe still hadn't seen it yet, but it sounded like it would be stunning from the description. They were going to have their girl's sleepover tonight, but Maggie had prom court duties after school again, so they moved it to Saturday night instead. Phoebe was okay with that since she could then still work her Saturday morning shift.

Thoughts of college were becoming very prominent with hearing about others getting their acceptance letters. She hadn't heard from any yet but knew it could be anytime now. She really wanted to make sure she was working to get some money to help pay for tuition. Phoebe heard a loud excited screech from a few lockers over.

"My mom just texted me! Ladies you are looking at the newest Firehawk!" Brittney screamed and clapped her hands as her friends jumped up and down around her. "Go Firehawks" they all shouted throwing their hands into the air wiggling their fingers. Phoebe had seen her sister, Anna, do this same move numerous times. It was supposed to look like flames. It actually did look pretty cool when all the cheerleaders did it together at the end of a routine. Right now, it just made Phoebe want to cringe. She wondered if she got her letter in the mail. She would just have to wait until she got home from work to find out. Even if there was a letter for her, her mom made a strict policy about opening only mail that belong to yourself.

"I can't wait to tell Jasper," Phoebe heard Brittany say. Her heart began to race. "I know he will be so excited. Remember how he was wishing me good luck and was saying how much he was hoping we would be going to school together next year?" Phoebe felt her face flush. Had Jasper and Brittany really been talking? She knew games had been getting more and more intense for Tommy and Jasper, so she hadn't contacted or heard from either of them since they were over on Sunday. Maybe, she hadn't heard from him because he was hanging out with Brittany?

"He will totally be thrilled. You should text him now to let him know. Maybe, we could celebrate after church on Sunday?" Charlotte said. Phoebe didn't want to even look over at them. She knew her face would expose exactly how she was feeling.

"Yes, I bet he would love to take me out!" Brittany slammed her locker door and the girls walked past Phoebe's locker. "Go Firehawks!" Brittany wiggled her fingers at Phoebe as she passed by, letting her long hair cascade down her back as she threw back her head and laughed. Now Phoebe felt nauseous, she just wanted to get out of school and head home to bed. She picked up her schoolbag and walked slowly to the parking lot with hopes not to have to run into Brittany and crowd again. When Phoebe reached her car, she felt her phone vibrate in her pocket. The caller ID said it was from the Bakery.

"Hello?" Phoebe answered as she threw her backpack onto the passenger seat.

"Hi, Phoebe," Mrs. Barker started. "I hope you aren't answering the phone while driving."

"No, I was just getting into my car. I should be there in a few minutes." Phoebe laughed. Mrs. Barker was so lovely. She was like another grandma always looking out for Phoebe.

"That's actually why I am calling. I am glad I caught you." That didn't sound good. Phoebe remained silent waiting for Mrs. Barker to finish. "A pipe burst this afternoon. The bakery had flooded."

"Oh, my goodness! Is everything going to be, okay?"

"Yes, dear, I believe so. However, there is quite a mess, so we had to shut down. You don't need to come in this afternoon, but if you could still come early tomorrow morning that would be just wonderful."

"Absolutely. Are you sure there isn't anything I could help with right now?" Phoebe asked.

"No, dear. I have the plumbers here, so we would just be in their way. We will still close tomorrow; but if you could come in to help with baking and restock that would be so helpful. I had to throw out all the goods, but I was able to schedule a delivery from the grocery tonight to restart."

"I am so sorry to hear that you lost everything. I will be there early tomorrow to help get everything going." Phoebe climbed into her car and shut the door.

"Thank you, Phoebe. See you tomorrow, dear," Mrs. Baker said ending their conversations. Phoebe sat in her car for a few minutes. Now that she didn't have to go to work, she really wasn't sure what she wanted to do. Should she go home and see if she got an acceptance or rejection letter like Brittany did? Or should she head over to the college and watch Anna finish the last of her practice before having to pick her up? She could also just go to a coffee shop. Sitting in her car holding the steering wheel while the parking lot emptied for the weekend, she decided she shouldn't put off the nagging voice in her head about going home to check the mail. She turned on her car, took a deep breath, and headed home.

"Hello?" Phoebe called out as she entered the front foyer. She placed her bag on the stairs to bring it up later. "Mom?" She called out.

"In the kitchen, Pheebs!" Mrs. Anderson answered. She was pulling fresh oatmeal cookies out of the oven. They were Phoebe's favourite. "I thought you had to work after school today?" Phoebe's mom said, placing warm gooey cookies on the cooling rack. Phoebe's mouth watered as she watched her mom put each one down.

"I was, but the bakery flooded. I guess a pipe burst. Poor Mrs. Barker said she lost all the food; but I am going to go in tomorrow to help get things rolling again. I hope the damage isn't too bad."

"Oh my, that's horrible; but it doesn't sound like it can be extensive if you are able to go in tomorrow. Please, let Mrs. Barker know if she needs any more help, I am here."

"Thanks, Mom, I will let her know." Phoebe gulped and felt nerves rush through her body. "Did you by any chance pick up the mail today?" She rubbed her hands on her jeans trying to get the nervous tickles in her palms to go away.

"I did." Her mom nodded pointing to a pile of mail on the counter by the patio door. "There seems to be quite a number of pieces for you, actually." Phoebe took a deep breath and picked up the pile of mail to sort. There were three envelopes, one from each of the colleges that she had applied to. Dover Christian College, UCLA and Fendry.

"They all came at once." She blinked looking at all three pieces.

"I know, I was shocked too. Are you going to open them?" Her mom asked in a calm soothing voice. Phoebe silently said a prayer. *Jesus, I know you are here with me in this moment and in every moment moving forward. Please, help me to know the place you want me to go.* She knew if she waited a few more seconds, she would freak out. She ripped open Dover Christian College first.

"I got in!" Phoebe screamed. Dover Christian wasn't her top pick, and it was far from home, but at least she felt some peace knowing that she was going to college after graduation. She immediately opened UCLA. It was her first back up. "I was wait listed". Phoebe scanned the letter. That didn't mean she wouldn't get in, but what if she didn't? That would mean she would have to move away from her family. It was a four-year program. She would practically miss Tabby growing up. Could they even afford all those fees. She felt like her mind was spinning out of control.

"Are you okay, sweetie?" Her mom came over and started rubbing her back.

"What if I don't get into Fendry, Mom? I would have to move away. Can we even afford that?" Phoebe start to feel her hands shaking.

"That's not something to worry about right now. We will sort that all out, if we have to. Remember that God is in control. Sometimes he works in really mysterious ways. He is always there for you. Come on now, open your letter from Fendry, Pheebs." Mrs. Anderson tapped on the letter with big red letters saying Fendry College on it.

"I am so nervous."

"It is normal to feel that way, sweetie. You can do this." Phoebe looked at her mom and tried to smile. She was so glad that her mom was with her. She opened the letter and slowly pulled the thin piece of paper out. She felt her face go hot and cold all at the same time.

"So?" Phoebe's mom gave her a poke coaxing her back to reality.

"I did it. I got in." Phoebe felt a huge wave of relief flood over her; it was followed by a gentle sense of peace. Almost as someone was whispering to her. In that instant, Fendry College is where she would call home. It didn't matter that it was close to home, although it was a benefit, God wanted her there. She couldn't explain how she knew, but she was confident it was where she needed to be. "I got in!" she shouted again. Her mom gave her a tight squeeze.

"I knew you could do it! Celebratory cookies!" Mrs. Anderson placed two cookies down in front of Phoebe and clapped her hands. "Oh, I am just so thrilled for you. You worked so hard, and it paid off. Congratulations, Pheebs! It will be so nice to have you home still, I mean if that is where you decide to go. You could still go to either Dover or UCLA as well."

"Thanks, Mom. Fendry is where I am going to go. I know that is where I belong." The Andersons were supportive parents. She knew if she wanted to go to one of the other Colleges her parents would help her achieve that, no matter the cost. Phoebe felt proud of herself and even more thankful that such a large unknown was now clear. "I am going to go call Dad and text the girls." Phoebe picked up the cookies and headed to find her phone. "Hey, how did you know that I would need celebratory cookies?" Phoebe asked her mom.

"Well, I knew you would get in, but when I saw all three envelopes, I knew you would also be stressed. Just in case they couldn't be celebratory cookies, they could have also been consolation cookies." This made both women laugh. "I am super happy that I was right in making celebratory cookies."

"Me, too." Phoebe beamed back at her mom.

Saturday morning came way too fast. All of the Andersons had come together to celebrate Phoebe's acceptance letter to Fendry and her decision to accept. Mr. Anderson had brought home pizza with all of her favourite toppings and Tabby even let her have the pick of movies to watch. Phoebe knew staying up late with her family would make it hard to get up the next morning, but in the moment she didn't care. Now that it was the crack of dawn, she was regretting her decision. She pulled on some sweats, thankful that there would be no customers at the bakery today. Arriving at the bakery, Phoebe pulled her car around the back and slipped in the side door. When she entered, she saw the "sorry we are closed" sign hanging on both the back and front doors.

"Hello?" She called out. The lights were on, but the rest of the shop was quiet.

"Hey," came a deep voice from the office making Phoebe jump. "Sorry, Phoebe, I didn't mean to scare you," laughed Cole. "Mrs. Barker is just picking up some supplies and said she would be right back.

"Oh, okay. I didn't know you were coming in today, Cole; I wasn't expecting your voice." Phoebe took off her bag, placing it on the office chair facing the small desk. "How bad is it?" She moved to look around the kitchen prep area and then to the check-out counter.

"Not that bad, actually. Mrs. Barker was right on top of it and now it is literally just the food prep that needs to be done. She called me to let me know not to come in yesterday. I told her I would come in today and help when she said it would just be you and her making food for opening on Monday." Cole looked at Phoebe with a bright smile. Normally, Phoebe wouldn't think anything of it, but since their last conversation about Jasper, Cole made her feel a little uncomfortable. "Want some coffee?" he asked.

"That would be great thanks." Cole continued to watch Phoebe. She twisted her hair up and wrapped an elastic around it, trying to ignore his gaze. "Did Mrs. Barker leave a list of things she wanted to get started on?"

"Yeah, just over there on the counter." Cole pointed to the sheet of paper next to a large mixer. Phoebe started to prep for the cinnamon buns that were on the top of the list. She knew they were a favourite for mornings. She could hear Cole shuffling around behind her, but she kept focusing on her task. She didn't know why or couldn't explain it but she just felt unease being with Cole. Her mom would often tell the girls that intuition and gut feelings could sometimes be the Holy Spirit talking to them and to not ignore those feelings. Was she just overreacting though because the comments he made about Jasper upset her?

"I am back!" Mrs. Barker called out form the side door. Phoebe put down the measuring cup she was using for flour to go help Mrs. Barker with the bags she was holding. "Good morning, Phoebe, thank you again for coming to help. I am so thankful for both you and Cole. You are both an answer to prayer. I promise if we can get stuck into it, we won't be here long.

"It's not a problem at all, Mrs. Barker; both Phoebe and I are so happy to help. It's not the first time I have been called an answer to prayer," Cole whispered the last part so only Phoebe had heard him. He handed her a coffee, smiling like a fox, then took the bags from Mrs. Barker. Phoebe was happy to help and happy to be able to keep her hours, but she didn't like Cole speaking for her.

"Lovely. Shall we get going?" Phoebe followed behind her.

Mrs. Barker took control as soon as she stepped in the door. She was correct, by noon they had completed all the baking that they had hoped for and more. Phoebe was wiping down the counters when Mrs. Barker excused herself to her office. Cole was sweeping up the floors.

"So, Pheebs," Cole said as he started sweeping closer and closer to where she was standing. "Do you have any plans tonight? There is a party on campus tonight my friends are throwing. I can totally get you on the list." His controlling gaze and smile were back. It felt like his eyeballs had some sort of weird hold on her.

"Thanks for the invite, but I have some friends coming over and staying the night." Phoebe continued to clean around the mixers and with her rag.

"Oh, that's cool. They could come too. There is going to be a couple of kegs and there is always a ton of shots to go around." Cole was now just holding onto his broom and using it to lean against. His hair flopping over his eyes.

"Thanks, but we are all under aged. I think we will have to pass."

"Oh, my friends totally don't care about underage, if that is what you are worried about. I'll give them your name and if you have any trouble at the door just tell them I invited you." He winked at Phoebe. Thankfully, she had finished wiping the counters clean and was ready to get her stuff to leave.

"Thanks, Cole. I don't think we will be able to make it." She was trying to be polite, but his insistence was really starting to get on her nerves. "Mrs. Barker, I am headed out now or is there anything else I can do for you?" Phoebe grabbed her bag as quickly as she could in hopes that Cole would get a hint.

"No, dear. Thank you again for your help. I am so happy with the progress." Mrs. Barker waved Phoebe off. Her genuine smile made Phoebe feel at ease, as opposed to Cole's.

"No problem at all. See you next week." With that Phoebe scurried out the door towards her car. She was just about to get inside when she heard her name called out. She grimaced. Was she going to have to snap at Cole for him to get the idea? She tried to avoid him as much as possible this morning and just told him no several times in regard to the party invite. She stood up straight and turned around ready to tell him to buzz off.

"Hey! We thought that was your car!" It was Tommy and Jasper. Tommy was hanging out the truck window, waving like a madman as Jasper pulled into the parking spot beside her car.

"Hey, guys!" Phoebe took a deep breath and felt the tension leave her shoulders, immediately.

"Are you okay?" Tommy asked, hopping out of the truck. You looked like you were ready to shoot laser beams out your eyes when you turned around?" Jasper walked over with a concerned look on his face as well.

"Oh, yeah, sorry. It was a late-night last night and an early morning. I guess I am just tired." Phoebe tried to laugh it off as Tommy gave her a tight squeeze. Jasper's face hardened as he looked over her shoulder.

"Hey," Jasper nodded. Phoebe turned around to see Cole standing by the side door watching them.

"Jasper, Tommy." Cole nodded in their direction. "See you tonight, Pheebs." Cole plastered on a fake smile and waved as he walked around the building to the front.

"Do you have to work again tonight? We saw the notice on the door about a flood. We came down in hopes of some treats and to see you of course." Tommy bumped her with his hip raising his eyebrows. It immediately made Phoebe burst into laughter.

"No, he invited me to a party tonight on campus," she mumbled. "Sorry about the treat's guys, but the store is open Monday, so you can get your fix then if you are in town."

"You're not going to that party, are you?" Jasper's strong firm voice surprised Phoebe. It was a drastic change from how he usually talked to her.

"Um, no, I have some friends coming over tonight. Parties aren't really my thing." Phoebe looked into Jasper's chocolate brown concerned eyes.

"That's good. Those parties aren't really a great place to be," Tommy replied, looking in between Phoebe and Jasper, they could not break each other's eye contact. "So, now that we've got that covered…" Tommy said awkwardly, "we actually need to get going. Your dad is going to help us rip up the rest of my aunt's backyard with his machine. He said he would meet us there at one."

"Oh, wow, he didn't mention that. I am glad it worked out that he could help. Sorry again about the lack of treats," Phoebe said, finally able to move her eyes from Jasper's concerned face to Tommy's full covered grin.

"Aw, that's okay, Wally Pheebs. Seeing you is a treat too." Tommy gave her a tight squeeze. His corny comment made both Phoebe and Jasper laugh.

"We are going to church with Tommy's aunt tomorrow. Will you be there?" Jasper asked. Phoebe connected with his dark eyes again.

"Yeah, I will be there." She was surprised that Jasper asked her. He was usually so quiet when they were in person, especially, when other people were around. She felt like she talked to him most when they were texting. It was kind of nice that he was showing interest in person.

"Awesome! We will see you then. Have a great day, Pheebs." Tommy jumped into the truck and gave a wave. Then pulled out his phone. It looked like he was sending a message to someone.

"See you tomorrow morning then. Have fun with your friends tonight." Jasper smiled his lopped sided grin at her. Phoebe felt her heart do a little flip.

"Sounds good. Good luck with the backyard." Jasper waved and climbed into the truck. Phoebe watched them pull away, as she got into her own vehicle. She was exhausted. There was so much going on just in the past twenty-four hours her head felt like it was swirling. Maybe, she could sneak in a nap before the girls came over for a sleep over tonight. She knew if she didn't, she would crash early. She really wanted to be able to reconnect with Maggie and Jenn. They hadn't been able to spend much time together recently at all.

By the time Phoebe got home, avoiding a nap wasn't even an option. She was so tired. She quickly said hello to her mom who did say that Mr. Anderson was off to help Tommy's aunt with the backyard. She also let Phoebe know that Mary, Anna, and Tabby went grocery shopping for her and would be back later. So now was actually the perfect time for a nap. Phoebe slowly climbed the stairs and sank into her bed. Her head was whirling with thoughts of acceptance and her decision to attend Fendry. Then add in her experience with

Cole and the short run in with Tommy and Jasper. Also, she just started to focus on growing a stronger relationship with God. She could feel Him moving in her life. She was beginning to feel more confident in herself and the path of self-discovery she was on. However, if she tried to dissect everything right this second sleep would elude her. Letting it all go for the moment, she drifted to sleep within seconds.

Chapter Fourteen

"Pheebs?" A soft voice and gentle hand rubbed Phoebe's back.

"Maybe, we should try something more aggressive, like loud music or a wedgie!" Phoebe recognized Jenn's cackle immediately and started to roll over onto her back.

"Don't even think about it," she said as she sat up to look at her two best friends. "When did you guys get here? What time is it?" Phoebe asked rubbing her face, trying to wake up.

"Well, we got here about fifteen minutes ago and it's just after 4:00. We would have been here sooner, but Jenn locked her keys inside the running car. How? I am not exactly sure," Maggie said sighing and trying to hide her laugh.

"It was an accident! I am not talking about it anymore," Jenn shrieked. "We have been trying to wake you for the past ten minutes, but you were seriously dead to the world."

"Sorry, I was so tired. We were up late last night celebrating and then I had an early shift this morning." Phoebe sat up and moved over so both Jenn and Maggie could squish onto her small single bed. "I am good, now. I am glad this finally worked out."

"Me, too! So, ladies what should we do tonight?" Jenn asked, enthusiastically clapping her hands.

"We actually got invited to a college party." Phoebe laid back on her pillow. She knew both Maggie and Jenn would not want to go, just like her, but it would be fun to see their response.

"Um, what?" Jenn arched her eyebrow.

"Yeah, spill, what are you talking about?" Maggie grabbed one of Phoebe's pillow and hugged it closely. Phoebe dished out all the details of the day about both Cole and Tommy and Jasper's quick visit.

"It sounds like Jasper is not a fan of Cole and vice versa," Maggie concluded.

"Totally," agreed Phoebe. "I kind of wonder why."

"Well, I for one am not interested in going to a party with Cole and his friends. The one time I was in the bakery, he gave me the willies too." Jenn wiggled her fingers at her friends making all of them laugh. "I do find it interesting that Tommy and Jasper keep coming to see you at the bakery, like every shift."

"Not every shift! And it's just because Tommy loves food so much."

"Sure..." both Maggie and Jenn said at the same time. All the girls laughed, and Phoebe chucked the pillow she was laying on at Jenn.

"Well, speaking of boys..." Maggie let out a breath. I have been meaning to tell you guys..." She rubbed her hands on her jeans, pausing. "I was actually asked to Prom."

"What? That's so exciting. By whom?" Jenn squealed.

"Oliver Miller, and before you say anything else, I kind of said yes."

"What? How did that happen? Tell us everything!" Jenn was practically bouncing off the bed. Phoebe was trying to show excitement for her friend, but she couldn't help but feel a little disappointed knowing that they would not all be going together like they had originally planned.

"Well, we have been doing a lot of prom court stuff together. He is actually really funny and nice and really smart. We just started connecting on a lot of things." Phoebe could tell Maggie was feeling a little hesitant to tell them. Oliver was one of the LIONS, also meaning he was one of the "cool kid" guys that hung around Brittney.

"Maggie, that's great. Aren't you excited?" Jenn questioned.

"Yeah, I am, actually. I just know we had planned to go all together. I didn't want to upset you guys. It's just that I kind of am interested in him and prom is a once in a lifetime experience." Phoebe knew Maggie was right, it was a once in a lifetime experience, and she also knew Maggie. Her best friend would never hurt her on purpose. Also, she had never even shown interest in someone as long as Phoebe had known her. Oliver must be decent. She should give him a chance.

"We are happy for you, Mags. Oliver must be great, if you like him. And we will see each other there; it's not like we are going to different places." Phoebe smiled at her friend. She wanted Maggie to be happy. On the bright side, she could still go with Jenn.

"Thanks guys." Maggie immediately started beaming. "I think you guys will really like him, once you get to know him better. He already said that we could sit with you guys instead of his buddies, so we'll definitely be together still."

"Well, I am glad you guys are okay with dates, because I was kind of asked too." Maggie spun around to look at Jenn who was nibbling on her fingernails.

"What?" It was now Maggie who was squealing. Phoebe felt like her head was spinning in shock. She felt like she just got over one major hurdle with her acceptance to Fendry, but now prom felt like it was another huge obstacle she was going to be facing.

"Josh from track asked me yesterday afternoon. I told him I would have to ask you guys first because we were planning on going together." Jenn continued to bite her nails, but Phoebe could see the smile hiding behind her fingers. "Pheebs, I know this would leave you without a date, so if you don't want me to say yes, I won't." Phoebe felt like her friend's hopeful stare was a fireball. That would mean she would have to go to prom solo. Yes, her friends would be there, but she would have to walk in by herself, sit at the table while they danced with their dates. She knew they wouldn't ever leave her out on purpose, but the truth was she was going to be the fifth wheel. Prom was not something that she was comfortable with now. Having a lack of confidence, going by herself was something that was going to be really difficult.

"Pheebs," Maggie snapped. Phoebe looked up at her. She knew what the right thing was to do but in this moment the fear and awkwardness of having to go by herself was making it really hard to do.

"Yes, of course, I want you to go with Josh. That's so exciting, Jenn! Like I said, we will still be together at Prom." Phoebe plastered on a fake smile as her two best friends squealed and bounced up and down on her bed. At least, they were excited, but now all Phoebe felt was dread.

"Girls!" Mrs. Anderson called from downstairs, "pizzas is here, and we have some more guests. Maggie and Jenn jumped off the bed talking about Prom dresses and plans in excitement. Phoebe slowly followed behind them. She was thankful her mom called them down so she could attempt to pull herself together. Prom wasn't her thing in the first place, but now it was starting to feel like a nightmare.

When the girls reached the table, both Maggie and Jenn had come to a complete halt in movement and conversation.

"Oh... My... Gosh..." Jenn said. Phoebe snapped out of her clouded mind and looked up. There, sitting at her dining room table was Tommy and Jasper.

"It's freaking Jasper Brown and Thomas Hernandez!" Jenn almost screamed in disbelief. This time Phoebe felt the same excitement as Jenn, but definitely was not showing it the same way.

"That's us," laughed Tommy. Making everyone else in the room chuckle too.

"I am a huge fan! Not as big as my dad. Oh man, would he ever be freaking out now. I can't wait to tell him. We watch or listen to every game. Can I get a picture; wait, I should go call him!" Jenn was talking so fast and waving her hands in the air. Thankfully, Mrs. Anderson came to the rescue for all their sakes and placed her hands on Jenn's shoulders to steady her.

"Jenn, why don't we have some pizza first. Then maybe the boys will agree to take a picture with you." Phoebe's mom calmly ushered all the girls to find a seat at the very squished table.

"Right, that sounds great." Phoebe could tell Jenn was trying to pull it together but was failing as she slipped into the seat across from Tommy still beaming at him like a wide-eyed creepy stalker.

"Tommy, Jasper, these are Phoebe's best friends, Jenn and Maggie," Mrs. Anderson explained.

"Hi," Maggie waved.

"GO FIREHAWKS!" shouted Jenn, pumping her fist in the air. Phoebe looked at Jasper. She had mentioned Jenn to him before and about how big of a fan she was. Jasper gave her a smile and she could tell he remembered the conversation too.

"Sorry about the tight fit around the table tonight, everyone, but company is always welcomed. We will just have to enjoy it a little closer today," Mr. Anderson stated from his usual spot at the head of the table. Phoebe looked around. In addition to her family of six there was Jenn, Maggie, Tommy, Jasper, and Andrew – Mary's boyfriend. That made a total of eleven people around an eight-seater table.

"We really appreciate you having us." Jasper's deep voice floated through the air.

"Yeah, my aunt only had bread left in the kitchen. She went to visit my mom this weekend. I think she is getting tired of looking at the mess outside," Tommy laughed.

"You boys did an amazing job out there today. We are happy to have you," Mr. Anderson stated. "Let's pray so we can eat the pizza before it gets cold." Mr. Anderson gave thanks for the food, for the company around his table, and at the end thanked the Lord again for Phoebe getting into Fendry.

"Amen!" They all said. The plates and pizza started to be passed around. Jasper looked at Phoebe.

"You got in?" he asked. His lopsided smile growing on his face.

"I found out yesterday." Phoebe returned the smile nodding her head.

"Congratulations. That's awesome. Are you going to accept?" he asked.

"Yeah, I am." Phoebe stated confidently.

"How did you come to the decision, if you don't mind me asking?" The table grew quiet. It was as if everyone also wanted to hear her answer Jasper's question.

"I can't really explain it. As soon as I opened the letter and saw that I was accepted, I felt this peace and comfort. I knew God was saying that was where He wanted me. I know that sounds crazy, but it's the truth." She shrugged her shoulders feeling a little uncomfortable with everyone looking at her. She never talked about stuff like this with her friends of family.

"You do sound crazy," Tabby laughed. Phoebe saw her mom open her mouth, probably to try and diffuse the situation, but Jasper broke the silence first.

"Actually, I had a similar experience when I decided to go to Fendry. It was an unexplainable pull towards Fendry College versus my others. I knew it was God who was telling me to go there." Everyone was quiet as they listened to him. "I think it is so cool how God can communicate with us in different ways. It was like Elijah in the bible. You know? Elijah went into the mountains seeking God. First, there was these crazy winds that were tearing down the mountains, but that wasn't God. Then there was an actual earthquake! Can you imagine being in a cave and feeling the earth violently shake beneath you? I would be terrified; but God wasn't in the earthquake, either." Everyone was captivated by Jasper as he was speaking. "Then there was a fire. Talk about crazy intense natural disasters happening. God wasn't in the fire, either. What followed was a soft whisper and that was God and Elijah knew it. God had a conversation with Elijah and told him where to go and what to do next. God could have come in showing how strong and almighty He is, but He chose to come in a whisper." Jasper smiled at Phoebe, she felt so connected to him in that moment and so thankful for his words. Everyone remained silent, not because it was an awkward moment but because they all were taking in what Jasper had just told them. Breaking the silence, Tabby turned to Tommy.

"Did God speak to you too, Tommy?" Tabby asked. She seemed to be genuinely interested and her teasing voice about the Lord guiding people had vanished.

"Oh no, not me. I didn't have that experience." Tommy shook his head. "I am one of eight kids in my family. As you can imagine putting eight kids through school would be a lot of money. Fendry gave me the best offer to go play for them, all expenses paid and a food plan. We all know how much I can eat. I am not sure they got their money's worth on that deal." They all laughed as Tommy patted his stomach and wiggled his eyebrows.

"I think those are both very noble and important information to base your decisions on. I am sure you made your families proud," Mr. Anderson praised both boys. Phoebe loved that her parents were getting to see this side of Jasper and even her sisters. She felt like all the rumours about him being a womanizer or a "typical college jock" would be put at bay.

"Have you heard anything from College's yet, girls?" Mrs. Anderson asked Maggie and Jenn.

"I am going to UCLA," Maggie stated. She got an early acceptance to the political science program and was thrilled.

"I haven't checked the mail yet." Jenn shrugged. She wasn't as concerned with getting in as Phoebe was. Jenn was most likely going to Fendry on a track scholarship.

The rest of dinner conversation flowed around the room. Phoebe mostly talked with her friends and her mom about college and potential classes they could take. Every once and a while, she would peek up at Jasper to find him and his lopsided grin smiling back at her. Butterflies fluttered inside her.

When the pizza was gone and the dishes were cleaned up, everyone had moved to the living room to chat. Tommy and Jasper agreed to take way too many photos with Jenn. Tabby had begun to instruct them to do really strange poses like all peeking out from the couch cushions or pretending to play catch.

"Now, you guys should each kiss one side of her cheek!" Tabby said holding up Jenn's phone to take the picture.

"Alright, I think these boys have done their duty, right Jenn?" Mr. Anderson stated.

"More than enough!" Jenn smiled. "Thanks, so much guys." She took her phone back from Tabby and they both sat down to flip through the pictures. Tabby pointed out all the ones she thought were best.

"Thanks so much again for having us," Jasper said, walking to Phoebe's dad to shake his hand. Tommy followed suit.

"Seriously, thank you. From me and my stomach!" Tommy laughed. "And thanks for your help with the machine. I think it would have taken us months to get that stump out."

"Anytime, boys." Mr. Anderson stood up to walk them out.

"Aren't you going to go say good-bye?" whispered Jenn.

"No, they are talking to my dad. That would be weird," Phoebe whispered back.

"You barely talked to Jasper. Don't you want to show him that you are interested?" Maggie leaned her head forward to get in on the conversation.

"Guys, I appreciate it, but Jasper is way out of my league."

"I don't think he feels that, judging from the way he was looking at you at dinner. And your little connection about God whispering to you both. That can't be a coincidence." Jenn wiggled her eyebrows.

"Oh, stop!" Phoebe laughed. A thrill of hope shot through her.

"See you, Andersons and friends, tomorrow at church!" Tommy called from the door before closing it on the way out.

Everyone dispersed after that. Mary and Andrew were off to see some animal documentary. Anna asked mom and Tabby if she could practice her manicures on them and Mr. Anderson pulled out his book, sitting down in his favourite chair for his after dinner reading session.

Hours later, Phoebe looked at the clock next to her bed. It was two in the morning. Thank goodness she had taken that nap. The girls had talk about everything from exams, college, work, and then prom and more prom. All the excitement her friends were feeling was starting to rub off on Phoebe. They had promised to make sure she didn't feel left out and wouldn't be by herself all night. They also all agree to get their hair done at the salon together. Phoebe initially was planning on letting Anna do it but now she wanted to be with her friends. She could hear Maggie's soft breathing alternating with Jenn's snores. There was literally no floor space left in Phoebe's small room. She rolled over quietly to plug in her phone when she noticed there was a text message notification.

Jasper: Hey, I just wanted to say congratulations again on getting into Fendry. I know you were searching for answers. I am really glad you found them. ☺

Phoebe's heart started to pound. She looked to see what time he had messaged her. It was an hour ago. Should she message him back? She didn't want him to think she was ignoring him.

Phoebe: Thanks so much! I am really excited.

Her phone vibrated seconds after she hit send.

Jasper: You're up late. Did you guys end up going to that party?

Phoebe: No. Not my thing, remember? We were just catching up all night. We haven't had a girls' night in forever. It was nice. We got to talk about College, prom, and everything going on lately. It was non-stop planning mode for them.

Jasper: Not for you?

Phoebe: Not really. I am not as excited about prom as they are.

Jasper: Why not?

Phoebe's heart stopped. Was he secretly trying to figure out if she was going with someone? Or was she going to seem lame and pathetic admitting that no one had asked her? She decided to be honest. She always felt that she could be with Jasper and there would be no judgement.

Phoebe: I don't have a date. The three of us were supposed to go together but they were both asked this week. I have now become the fifth wheel.

Jasper: Maybe, someone will ask you.

Phoebe: I don't think so, but I am okay with just hanging out with my friends. How was the rest of your day?

Phoebe wanted to drop the prom talk. She had enough of it for the day and really didn't want any sympathy from her crush. They ended up texting for an hour about his day and plans for the summer. Jasper had let her know her dad offered him and Tommy a job at Anderson Care, since they were both planning on staying around for the summer and doing extra training with the baseball coaches. This had made Phoebe super excited and had high hopes that she would see him more often. He had also asked if she, Maggie, and Jenn wanted to go for lunch after church tomorrow. Phoebe said she would have to check with her dad first but would like to. Phoebe finally drifted off to sleep with thoughts filled with Jasper.

Chapter Fifteen

Sunday mornings in the Anderson house were usually chaotic but today it was extra. Adding two more females trying to use one small bathroom was a struggle. Plus, a very upset and stubborn Tabby on top of that, and it seemed like it was going to be impossible to get out the door in time. Somehow, they managed to do it. Phoebe was allowed to ride with Jenn who drove both her and Maggie to Phoebe's house the day before. She was glad she was not in the van with the rest of the Andersons, as Tabby was pitching a fit about not being allowed to wear lipstick again. The girls hustled into church and sat down with the rest of Phoebe's family. The music had already started so Maggie and Jenn slid in next to Anna, leaving Phoebe at the end of the row. She smoothed out the hem of her yellow dress with white daisies on it. This dress made her feel light and airy. Today, she let her brown hair hang down naturally. When she got dressed this morning, Jenn made a remark on how she was getting all spiffy for Jasper. Phoebe tried to brush it off, but in reality, the girls knew that more effort was put in than normal for that reason. She scanned the room to try and see if Jasper and Tommy were there when the worship leaders asked the congregation to sit down. Finally, she spotted them near the front sitting next to Brittney and some other girls from the college and careers group. Phoebe watched as Brittney tugged on Jasper's arm and whispered in his ear. Her gut retched with jealous.

The remaining of the service, Phoebe found herself just watching Brittney and Jasper. Most of the time, there were just sitting there listening, but there were a couple of glances between the two of them. Phoebe had no idea what Pastor Moore talked about. When the service finished, she slumped behind her family and friends, no longer feeling cute and airy like she had before.

"Hey, Andersons and friends," Phoebe heard Tommy's upbeat voice call out as they gathered in the gym for coffee. This happened once a month at the church. There would be tables set out for everyone with coffee, tea, or juice. There would also be a light snack. The Anderson's would always go. Mr. Anderson stated the importance of church community.

"Tommy, wonderful to see you this morning," Mrs. Anderson said, giving him a quick hug. "Alright girls, we are only going to stay an hour or so. If you see Tabby, please, make sure she knows we are leaving at noon. I need to go and see if they need help in the kitchen." Mrs. Anderson bustled away.

"We actually need to get going, Pheebs," Jenn said. "My dad wanted to have lunch with my uncles today. Thanks for having us." Phoebe had asked if they could all go out for lunch with Jasper earlier this morning, but Jenn let her know that she had other plans. Mr. Anderson also said they couldn't this time because of the after-church coffee time. Jenn and Maggie both gave big hugs to everyone, including Tommy. Jenn's face turned beat red when she let go of him.

"I am glad it worked out. See you tomorrow at school." Phoebe waved good-bye to her friends. Mary had already disappeared somewhere after she said her good-byes, so it was just Anna, Tommy, and Phoebe left standing together.

"You ladies want to come sits with J and I? We are sitting over there." Tommy pointed to Jasper who was sitting next to Brittney laughing. They were at a table with the rest of the girls who they had sat with during the service. There didn't look to be enough spots left at the table for all three of them.

"Sure!" Anna smiled and headed right over to the table. Phoebe wished she had that much confidence. Anna could walk right up to any group of people and fit right in. She was always welcomed. Phoebe did not have the same experience.

"I think I am going to go help in the kitchen. I told my mom I would this morning when I found it was coffee time today." That was a lie. She just really didn't want to have any awkward moments, especially in front of Jasper with Brittney. Her face heated just thinking about it.

"Cool," Tommy said and left her to go sit next to Anna.

Phoebe actually enjoyed the hour of making coffee with the elderly ladies in the kitchen. They were always so thrilled to have her there and seemed so invested in what was going on in her life. They asked her about her future plans, which Phoebe excitedly divulged her acceptance to Fendry into the education program. She felt so confident in her answers and her path moving forward, which was a huge change from a few months ago. *Now if she could only feel that confident about going to prom by herself, and her relationship with Jasper,* she thought. All the ladies had shared congratulations for her acceptance and encouragement when they found out about her prom predicament. Phoebe loved the feeling of community and support from them. She was placing out the last tray of cookies on the table when she felt someone tap her on her shoulder.

"Hey, can I have one of those," Jasper's deep voice filled Phoebe's ears. She turned to his chocolate brown eyes and lopped sided smile.

"Oh, sure. It's the last tray so grab a few. Especially if you have to share them with Tommy," she joked.

"That's probably not a bad idea," Jasper laughed grabbing three cookies. "It was really nice of you to help out in the kitchen. I would have offered but one of the ladies didn't think I would have fit in. I was shooed away."

"You actually tried to come in?" Phoebe raised her eyebrows in shock.

"Yeah, I mean I would have gotten first dibs for all the cookies and avoided having to share with Tommy," Jasper laughed. "But also, Tommy told me you went in there." Phoebe's heart leaped.

"Oh." She didn't know what else to say.

"I was hoping we would have been able to hang out a bit more." Phoebe could not believe her ears. He had never been this forward with her before. She had hoped since meeting Jasper he would say something like this to her but now that it had happened, she didn't know how to respond. She nodded her head in agreement.

"Tommy and I won't be able to come next weekend because we have our last away game of the season, but I think the weekend after that we will be finishing up his aunt's place. Maybe, we could hang out then." Phoebe couldn't tell if he was asking her out as a date or if he wanted to just get together as friends. Again, she couldn't come up with the words to say, so she nodded her head in agreement.

"I'd like that," she finally mustered. Jasper's crocked grin appeared on his face and the little smile lines formed around his eyes.

"Yo, I hope those cookies are for me!" Tommy said, grabbing them out of Jaspers hands.

"See, this is why I should have tried harder to help in the kitchen," Jasper laughed. You could tell the bond that Jasper and Tommy had was more of a forever brotherhood than just teammates or friends.

"Sorry man, you know what sweets do to me." Tommy licked his lips and took a large bite of the cookie. "The girls were asking if we would go for lunch with them. I said I would have to ask you." Jasper looked over at the table where they were sitting. Brittney and her friends were gathering up their belongings and it looked like they were hugging Anna good-bye. "Anna mentioned that you guys couldn't make it out today," Tommy told Phoebe.

"If you want to go, we can. I just have to be back at school by two. I am meeting with one of my TA's." Jasper shrugged. Phoebe secretly wanted him to tell Tommy he didn't want to go. She didn't want Jasper to be spending any more time with Brittney, as petty as that was.

"Okay, let's just go for a quick burger with them because we have no food in the dorm, and we won't have time to go to the caff in between."

"Sure." Jasper grabbed one more cookie off the tray, shaking it in front of Tommy. "This one is for me, okay?" Tommy threw up his hands in agreement.

"All yours. See you in a couple of weeks, Wally Pheebs?" Tommy came over and gave Phoebe a side hug. "Maybe, I'll try to come to the bakery and get some goodies for the away game." He rubbed his hands together. Phoebe loved how genuine Tommy was.

"Sounds good. I am only working a few times this week, but the shop will be back open tomorrow."

"Jasper, are you guys coming?" Brittney slinked over to them and linked her arm with Jasper. She completely ignored Phoebe, acting like she and Jasper were the only ones there. Phoebe wanted to swat her hands away from him like an angry cat.

"Yeah, we can only grab some fast food. I have to be back at school, soon." Brittney started dragging Jasper out of the gym. Tommy followed behind them, leaving Phoebe alone with just a few cookies left on the plate.

Chapter Sixteen

Every senior, including Phoebe, was bustling around working on projects, getting ready for prom, which was two weeks away, or studying for exams. Phoebe was jealous of her lower-level student body. They all seemed to be more relax as they prepared for summer break. Phoebe found her new form of communication with friends and family was texting. She was either at school, work, or studying in her room. Phoebe also started texting with Jasper more and more each day. It began with both of them initiating conversations asking about each other's day or just saying a quick hi. Now the messages had become deeper in getting to know each other. She told him all about her ideas of becoming a grade two teacher, her love of dogs (but Tabby was allergic). She even felt safe enough to be honest and tell him how she felt like she would never live up to her sisters. In turn, Jasper explained the pressures he felt playing baseball, how it was his father's dream for him to go pro but he wasn't sure it was his. They also bantered back and forth and told each other meaningless facts about themselves. For example, Phoebe hated yogurt and Jasper secretly loved musicals. Phoebe found herself looking more and more forward to his messages and would pull out her phone quickly to check if it was him when she felt it vibrate. Jasper had messaged her during her last period, saying they were boarding the bus for Fendry's last away game. Phoebe sneaked in a good luck message, while her teacher was writing on the board.

"I am so excited! Sorry that you can't come with us, hon," Brittney started saying to her group of friends that followed her to her locker after class. "I told Tommy we were coming, and he was super excited. He said they always love having support at away games. I told him not to tell Jasper. I want it to be a surprise. I know he will love it that I am there. I even got one of his jerseys!" Brittney giggled and closed her locker. She made eye contact and wiggled her fingers in her signature good-bye wave to Phoebe as she and friends walked away. It was moments like these that made Phoebe question her feelings and relationship with Jasper. *How was he feeling about her? Was he sending the same kind of messages to Brittney?* Phoebe felt like there is no way she could compare to Brittney, a cheerleader, stunningly beautiful and she also had way more experience with guys, compared to Phoebe's virgin lips. It sure seemed like Brittney was under the impression that her relationship with Jasper was becoming more than a friendship. Maybe, she knew things Phoebe didn't. Maybe Phoebe was reading into everything due to her lack of experience. Everything felt so confusing and tangled. Flustered and a bit annoyed at Jasper, Brittney and herself, Phoebe jumped into her car to head to her shift at the Bakery. After work she had to pick up Anna from her cheerleading practice.

"Let it go," Phoebe whispered to herself. The drive didn't take long to get to work. Phoebe was able to distract her thoughts to other things she needed to take care of, clean the car, finish her biology paper, and pick out shoes to go with her prom dress. She was glad she decided on the green one that Anna a picked up for her a few weeks ago. It was now sitting in her parents closet and Phoebe was getting pretty excited to wear it, but still terrified of having to attend by herself. Anna had actually offered to do Maggie and Jenn's hair, instead of them all having to find a time slot at the salon together. Both Maggie and Jenn would then be picked up from Phoebe's house by their dates.

Phoebe placed her bag down in her employee cubby and headed out to the front of the bakery. There stood Cole, giving a large smile and wink to a junior Phoebe recognized from her school.

"Hey, Pheebs," Cole said after ringing through the girl's purchased. The girl blushed and returned to a table of her giggling friends.

"Hey," Phoebe replied tying on her apron. "Has it been busy today?"

"Not really. I would say that you could even go home, but I do enjoy having your company." Cole tried his smile and wink on Phoebe, she did not return it with the same enthusiasm as the junior girl from her school.

"Just so you know, that girl is a junior at my school, Cole." She nodded her head to the table of girls that were still sneaking glances at him. Phoebe could understand why. Maybe, a few years ago, she too would have fell under Cole's charming spell with his floppy hair and wide friendly grin. Several weeks ago, she was happy to work with Cole, but as she got to know him more, the more she realized he might not be the best company to be keeping.

"Oh, really? I was just being friendly with a customer. Are you jealous, Pheebs?" Cole wrapped his arm around Phoebe's shoulder and gave it a squeeze. She immediately shrugged it off and moved away.

"Not in the slightest. I just thought you should be aware of her age," Phoebe held her ground. No way she would let Cole intimidate her or let a girl fall for his tricks under her watch.

"Oh, good, I am so glad you are here. I have two large orders I would like you to pack for pick up early tomorrow morning. The counter has been slow today, so Cole you can stay upfront and stop hitting on those young girls." Mrs. Barker wagged her fingers at Cole. Phoebe couldn't help but let out a shocked laugh. Cole glared at her and headed back behind the counter to help out a gentleman waiting in line.

"Here is the list of the orders. One is for a women's church group, and one is for the Fendry Baseball team." Phoebe's head snapped up. "I thought you would be interested in packing that one. A very kind lady named Mrs. Hernandez called in the order. She said her nephew and friends loved the baked goods and she wanted to surprise them at their away game tomorrow."

"That's so nice of her. I know Tommy will love that." Phoebe took the lists looking both of them over. They were both quite large. She wasn't sure they had enough in stock to fill both of them. Almost as Mrs. Baker could read her mind, she let Phoebe know to pack the women's church group first, Mrs. Hernandez said she would take whatever was left in stock for the boys.

"Oh, and Phoebe," Mrs. Baker peaked her head out from her office, "I think a nice good luck note would be great to include in Fendry's order. Don't you?" Mrs. Barker didn't miss a beat. Phoebe wasn't sure how Mrs. Barker knew about her connection to the baseball team. She must have eyes everywhere. Mrs. Barker always seemed to be so aware about everything that was going on in the bakery, but also in her employees' lives. It wasn't creepy. It felt like it was a comfort of sorts. Like she knew she could always ask Mrs. Barker for help and would always receive advice and encouragement when needed.

"Sure, I can do that." Phoebe smiled at Mrs. Barker and then went to fill the orders. Thankfully, the front counter was a steady flow of college and high school students until close, so Phoebe was able to ignore Cole for the rest of her shift. She did end up writing a quick good luck message for the Fendry Baseball team and signed it "From your friends at Barker's Bakery". She decided to draw a small picture of a walrus at the end of the note. If Tommy or Jasper saw it, she hoped they would know it was from her.

When Phoebe picked up Anna from her cheer practice, she was on the phone talking about front twists and back handsprings. She finally hung up ten minutes from home letting out a huge sigh of relief.

"Sorry about that, we are trying to get the routine right for the game next weekend and it just isn't clicking for some of the girls. How was your day?" Phoebe unleashed the unfiltered version of her day to Anna. Phoebe was closest to Anna of all her sisters. She felt like she could tell her anything and not be judged by it.

"First, I am glad you came to your own conclusions about Cole. I forgot he worked at the bakery, or I would have told you to steer clear. He has been making his way through the college party scene and a lot of the fraternities and sororities are not happy with him. Many of those guys are on sports teams too, so that's probably why Jasper and Tommy had their backs up." Phoebe took all of her sister's information in. Everything from her intuition and personal encounters with Cole were clicking. "As for Brittney, I really don't think she means any harm." Phoebe rolled her eyes at Anna as if to say, yeah okay. "Really, Pheebs, I know she can come off harsh sometimes, but she is just trying to find her way, just like you are. As much as I know you hate to hear it, but a lot of girls are interesting it Jasper and even Tommy. It's not just you."

"I know," Phoebe sighed.

"I also know Mary warned you about cleat chasers and about falling for Jasper, but I support you. I am really enjoying getting to know both him and

Tommy. I feel like my perspective of them keeps getting better and better the more they come over. The rumours about them are definitely not true. I wonder if they know how people perceive them? It must be hard to have to try and break that narrative. I just want you to know that I am here for you. As mom always says, as hard as it is to believe sometimes, if God wants it to happen, it will. If it is in his plans then it is what is best for us." Phoebe had heard her mother say that so many times it was ingrained in her brain. There was a picture hanging in the kitchen that read: For I know the plans I have for you, declares the Lord, plans to prosper you, and not to harm you, plans to give you hope and future – Jeremiah 29: 11.

That night as Phoebe climbed into bed early, she reflected on her day and her conversation with Anna. She hadn't heard anything from Jasper since his message about getting on the bus. She decided that she would text him good luck early in the morning during her shift at the bakery. She prayed that God would help her to see the good in others, to help her to be herself and remember that whatever God had planned in her future would be for her good. She drifted off to sleep.

Barker's Bakery was apparently the place to be on Saturday morning. Mrs. Baker had to call in extra staff after the counter that was already depleted from the two orders Phoebe filled the day before was now nearly empty. Phoebe worked in the back with another high school student and Mrs. Baker making quick batches of cookies and squares. It wasn't normally what they would have today but the speed in which they could be made was the positive.

"Hey," Jordan, the college student who had been called in to help, popped her head back in the kitchen, "there is a Mrs. Hernandez here for a pickup order. I would look for it, but we are swamped!"

"Thanks, Jordan. Phoebe can you grab it and bring it out front?" Phoebe quickly wiped her hands on a towel and grabbed the boxes she had set aside yesterday. There was no mistaking who Mrs. Hernandez was, she and Tommy looked very similar with their olive skin, dark hair, and green shining eyes. Phoebe had met her once or twice at church as a child but had never had a conversation with her by herself.

"Hi, Mrs. Hernandez, here is your order. I packed it yesterday and everything you asked for was in stock; so there shouldn't be any issues." Phoebe smiled, placing down the large box of baked goods on the corner of the front counter.

"Phoebe, right?" She asked.

"Yes, I'm Phoebe Anderson."

"I should have known. You look just like your mother, but I also figured it was you from the way my boys talk about you. I considered them my boys while they are living away from their mamas. I make sure to take care of them." Mrs. Hernandez smiled.

"Oh," was all Phoebe could manage to reply with.

"All good things, I promise, especially Jasper which is interesting since he is quieter and more private. I guess I can't blame him considering the spotlight he has on his life. It seems to only be becoming more intense." She smiled at Phoebe shrugging. "Tommy also has good things to say, but he mostly talks about how good the cookies you made tastes. I swear that boy and his food. I pray for his wife and their grocery bill in the future." Both Mrs. Hernandez and Phoebe laughed because it was true. Tommy could eat someone out of house and home.

"He does have quite the appetite. I have been really enjoying getting to know them both." Phoebe felt like a diplomate as soon as those words came out of her mouth. Mrs. Hernandez cocked her eyebrow at Phoebe.

"Well, I was thinking the next time the boys are at my house for the weekend you should come over for dinner. In fact, I should have your whole family over. I owe your father for letting us use his machine in my backyard. Phew, what a disaster it was, but I know it will be all finished soon and worth the wait!"

"I know we would all love that, although you don't owe him or us anything. I think my dad loved being there to help. He loves demolition."

"Boys and their toys! My husband was the same way." Mrs. Hernandez seemed to go to another place mentioning her late husband. Phoebe's heart ached for her.

"Well, if we come for dinner then I will bring dessert!" Phoebe smiled.

"Sounds like a deal. Thank you so much for getting this order ready. I know all the boys will be thrilled. I better get going though because I have quite the drive to make before the game starts."

"Of course! Safe drive and please tell the boys good luck for me." Phoebe held open the bakery door for her so Mrs. Hernandez could exit safety. Phoebe returned to the kitchen to continue making goods for the shop. The rest of the morning did not slow down, but thankfully they were able to make enough pastries and cookies. Phoebe agree to work a few hours after her scheduled hours. Exhausted when she arrived home, all Phoebe wanted to do was sit in a hot shower and then have a quiet tea on the couch. Tabby had other ideas. She came bounding towards Phoebe the moment she walked in with their mother's phone in hand.

"Look, Jasper made the news!" Tabby held up the phone for her to see. There was a picture of Jasper at home plate swinging the bat. The title read *Fendry Firehawk Sends a Fireball Grand Slam*. "They won their game. Too bad it didn't help them make the playoffs. Phoebe took the phone from Tabby's hands and started to read the article. It had a lot of positive things to say about Jasper. Giving his stats and how he was a huge prospect for the major leagues if he continues playing as well as he did. As Phoebe scrolled down there was a picture of the team celebrating with their fans that "came all the way to support them". Phoebe couldn't help but smile when she saw Tommy hugging his aunt in celebration. She zoomed in on the picture. Her eyes growing wide. There beside Tommy was Jasper grinning. Around his neck wrapped a pair of arms that belonged to none other than Brittney. Phoebe gulped in some air. Her stomach twisted with jealousy. She wished it was her arms wrapped around Jasper in congratulations of his amazing grand slam. She handed the phone back to Tabby, telling her she needed to go shower. She needed to sort out her emotions.

"I am going to ask Jasper for an autograph on a baseball when he comes back. Do you know how much money that will be worth when he goes pro?" Tabby ran off to the kitchen, bouncing with glee. Phoebe shook her head at her little sister. She was such a spitfire. Of course, she would want an autograph to make a profit and not because Jasper was a friend.

Phoebe was finally able to have the tea on the couch after a late dinner that evening. Her mom sat across from her. The rest of the afternoon and evening was spent grocery shopping, organizing their week with who gets the car, and more. The two Anderson women sat silently together on the couch.

"Did Tabby show you the article about Jasper?" Mrs. Anderson broke the stillness.

"Yeah, she did. I am really happy for him. That must have been quite a hit."

"Must have been." Her mom sipped her tea. "Did you message him congratulations? I know you said you have been talking to him quite a bit." Phoebe had mentioned to her mom a couple of time that she was texting with Jasper.

"I haven't yet." Phoebe was still trying to process her feelings about the picture she saw of him and Brittney. The reminder from Mary and Anna about Jasper's popularity rang in her ears.

"Don't you think you should?" Her mom questioned.

"You're right. I just didn't want to interrupt any celebrations, but he is probably on the bus home now or in a hotel." Phoebe lied. She pulled out her phone.

"That was considerate of you." Her mom pulled her cup to her lips and took a sip again.

Phoebe: Hey hope I am not interrupting celebrations. Just wanted to say congratulations on your win! I read that you hit a grand slam. That's awesome!

Phoebe put her phone down. She did not expect him to text her back, nor did she want to get her hopes up.

"Is there anything going on between you and Jasper?" Phoebe's head shot up. Never had she spoken to her mom about boys before, but then again never had she been interest in someone enough or someone been interested in her. She often heard her mom talking to Anna about someone. Anna had been on plenty of dates but had always said she never had enough spark with someone. She had even heard Tabby talk to her mom about her crushes, but this conversation had never come up between them before. Phoebe wasn't sure what to say. "I only ask because you two seem to be texting a lot and he has been coming around a bit. Or am I totally off and you have feelings for Tommy? Tommy is lovely too!"

"Tommy is lovely, but he is not for me," Phoebe said in around about way to admit her attraction to Jasper.

"So, it is Jasper then?" Her mom confirmed for herself nodding.

"He is way out of my league, though. So, you have nothing to worry about." Phoebe replied.

"Why would you ever think he is out of your league?" Mrs. Anderson set her teacup down, now giving her full attention to Phoebe.

"Because I am just me. I am plain. I am not smart or driven like Mary, I am not outgoing and beautifully stunning like Anna, and I am not tenacious or funny like Tabby. Jasper is smart, kind, good looking and an amazing baseball player. I don't compare to any of the girls out there. I don't have anything special about me." Phoebe shrugged. She tried not to let a tear slip down her cheek, but it had escaped before she could catch it.

"Oh, Phoebe, I hate to know that this is the way you see yourself. When I look at you, I see a beautiful young woman that is smart, works hard to accomplish her goals, to provide for herself and help family. I see a woman that is strong in her convictions, that is constantly thinking of others and putting them before herself. You have a calming peace around you, but you also know how to have fun. Your heart exemplifies the love of Christ. If anything, I am not saying this just because I am your mom, Phoebe, you are too good for him. He would be so blessed to have you in his life." Phoebe smiled and rolled her eyes at her mom. Her mother's words had made her feel warm and appreciated, but she was her mom, didn't she have to say those things? "I mean it Phoebe; you are one of a kind. Sure, you are still finding yourself, but aren't we all? I don't know many other kids your age who would wake up early to help pay for school when their parents already said they would pay for it. You also are choosing a profession where you are going to have to have a kind loving heart every day with kids. I for one could not do that!"

"What are you talking about mom? You are great with kids, you had four girls!" Phoebe laughed.

"Yes, I did. I love you all very much, but four kids are enough for me. I don't want to watch anyone else's." Both Anderson women laughed hard together. Her mom was right. She was still finding herself and she had to give herself more grace and stop comparing herself to everyone else. God made her to be Phoebe, not her sisters or Brittney, or anyone else.

Phoebe still hadn't heard back from Jasper as she crawled into bed that night. For once that wasn't what was holding captive of her mind. She kept thinking of the qualities her mother had pointed out in her. She had to admit she was quite proud that someone else had noticed how hard she was working and how much she did want to help and take care of others. She prayed.

Jesus, please, give me the strength to be who I am, and who you have called me to be. I know I am still learning who that is, Lord. While I am figuring it all out, could you help me to stop comparing myself to others, it only makes my heart hurt and my thoughts become negative.

Please, give me confidence to live a life for you and please help me to find joy as I am on the road to finding Phoebe. Amen.

Chapter Seventeen

"Tabby, don't hit her on her head. You could actually hurt her." Mary's voice broke into Phoebe's subconscious.

"How else do you want me to wake her up? Everything you tried didn't work. Oh, I know, I'll go get a bucket of water!" Phoebe still felt like she couldn't open her eyes. Her body felt like a million pounds and her throat felt scratchy and hot.

"Phoebe, if you can hear me, you better open your eyes soon and sit up. Tabby is actually going to get a bucket of water. I don't think I will be able to talk her out of dumping it on you." Mary weight shifted on the bed.

Phoebe slowly opened her eyes and pushed herself into sitting position.

"Oh, man!" Tabby grumbled standing in the doorway with a big pot of water that they usually use for lasagna night. She stared Phoebe down before she left with water sloshing over the sides of the pot.

"Just in time," Mary snickered. "You okay, Pheebs?" Mary asked.

"I think so; my throat is a little sore, but I could have been sleeping with my mouth open."

"Maybe," Mary shrugged, looking at her intently. "You were really hard to wake up. We have to leave in ten minutes for church. Let me feel your head because you do look a little pale."

"You mean more than I usually do?" Phoebe laughed, but it caused a horse cough to follow it.

"You don't have a fever, but I think I'll go get mom." Mary got up swiftly. As Phoebe laid back down, she could hear Mary telling Tabby to go put the pot away because she could not dump water on Phoebe. She heard Tabby complaining all the way down the stairs. A few minutes later, mom appeared in her bedroom doorway.

"Hey, sweetie, Mary said you weren't feeling well." Her mom walked over to her bed, placing her palm on Phoebe's forehead just as Mary had done. "No fever yet. Is it just a sore throat?"

"Yeah." Phoebe's voice was just as scratchy as her throat felt.

"Okay, why don't you stay home from church today. I'll make you some tea and leave it on the counter. Hopefully, it isn't anything serious and just a case of getting run down. You have been doing a lot with exams, work, and prom all right around the corner." Phoebe nodded her head in thanks.

When Phoebe's family arrived back home after attending church without her, she felt a little better. The shower and tea had done her well and she was now sipping her second cup on the couch watching a rerun episode of Survivor. She had changed into a pair of matching sweats and pulled her long hair up into a bun straight from the shower. The peace and quiet that she was enjoying vanished quickly. Tabby had run over to show her the bookmark she made in Sunday school. Mrs. Anderson came to feel her forehead, relieved that she still did not have a fever and was feeling better than this morning. She then pulled Tabby away to clean up her shoes and help her make some soup for lunch. Anna slid down on the couch beside Phoebe, smiling.

"Hey," Phoebe whispered.

"Hi, yourself." Anna was grinning like a Cheshire cat.

"What?" this time her voice cracked causing her to cough.

"Well, I missed having you at church, but I wasn't the only one." Anna continued to grin like crazy. "Jasper was there." Phoebe felt her eyes widen as Anna grabbed her arm and squealed a bit. "I guess Mrs. Hernandez was allowed to give Tommy and Jasper a ride home last night after the game and they came to church with her! Jasper was asking me where you were. It was actually the first thing he said to me. Not even a hello." Phoebe felt her face redden and her heart speed up a bit.

"What did you..." She started to whisper but Anna cut her off.

"Tell him? The truth, that you weren't feeling well and had a sore throat, so you stayed home today. He said to tell you he hopes you feel better soon."

"Oh well, that was nice." Phoebe had to admit she was hoping for a little bit more, but she was excited that he was looking for her. Especially since, she hadn't heard from him since he boarded the bus before his game. A loud laugh came from the front door as Mary, Andrew, and her dad had walked into the house. They all moved to sit in the living room with Phoebe and Anna, so their discussion had ended there.

"Hey, Pheebs. Heard your throat isn't feeling too great. Want me to take a look?" Andrew asked already moving towards her spot on the couch. She knew if she said no, he would be insulted with all his interest and study in the medical field, so she just opened her mouth wide for him to look in. "Well, you don't have any signs of strep, which is good. I think your mom is right. Your body is probably just exhausted from everything going on. I think a day of movies and soup will do the trick." He gave her a wink as if to say, I got your back, and then sat back down next to Mary on the love seat.

"Thanks," Phoebe mumbled. The rest of the afternoon, Phoebe, Anna, Mary, and Andrew spent the day doing just as he said, watching movies. Mr. Anderson retreated downstairs to his office to get some paperwork done and Mrs. Anderson and Tabby went out shopping for some new church shoes. It was close to five when the doorbell rang. The four of them looked at each other in shock. None of them were expecting anyone, especially someone who would ring the doorbell. Any of Anna's or Phoebe's friends would walk right in. Her parents always had an open-door policy. They wanted everyone to feel welcome in their home just as Jesus made anyone feel welcome to come to Him. Phoebe loved that about her house and wanted to adopt that way of thinking when she had her own home. Mr. Anderson had come up from the study to answer the door. Anna peeked around the corner and immediately ran over to Phoebe. She pinched her cheeks hard.

"Ow! What was that for?" Phoebe swatted her away.

"Quick, put on some of my lip balm." Anna smashed some onto Phoebe's unexpecting lips. Mary and Andrew stared at them in confusion. Phoebe could see Andrew was trying to stifle his laugh at the sisterly antics.

"It's Jasper and Tommy," Anna whispered loudly just as the two boys walked into the living room.

"Hey, guys," Tommy laughed. It was clear that they had heard Anna's warning of their arrival.

"Hi!" they all said at once and then burst out laughing.

"Congratulations on your win. That hit was amazing Jasper. I watched it over a couple times online!" Andrew got up and shook Jasper's hand. He went to shake Tommy's, but he was holding a ginormous pot in his hands. Mr. Anderson came into the room and grabbed it from Tommy.

"My aunt heard from a certain someone," he glanced and smiled at Jasper, "that Wally Pheebs wasn't feeling too great, so she made a huge pot of her famous chili. She has taken quite a liking to you, Pheebs. She said you made her the teams' favourite auntie!"

"That was so sweet of her," Phoebe whispered smiling widely. She tried to ignore the fact that she probably looked absolutely horrible and potentially had large pinch marks on her cheeks from Anna.

Why don't you boys go ahead and grab a seat there. I'll warm this chili up and call mom to let her know we don't have to worry about dinner tonight. You boys will join us, won't you?" Phoebe could not believe what was happening. This moment felt surreal for so many reasons. Jasper and Tommy should still be away or back at their dorm not here in their living room. And her father was actually inviting them to stay for dinner to a meal that another woman had made her because she was sick.

"That would be awesome. Thanks!" Anna moved off the couch and onto the floor in front of Mary, leaving room for both Jasper and Tommy to sit beside Phoebe. Andrew jumped right into conversation about the baseball game the boys just got back from. He was asking all sorts of questions, which both Jasper and Tommy gracefully answered. When Tommy was answering a question about one of the plays the other team had made, Jasper leaned over to Phoebe.

"How are you feeling?" he asked.

"Um, okay, better than this morning. It's just a sore throat. Thanks for bringing over the chili." She smiled at him.

"No problem. Mrs. Hernandez's chili is a miracle worker on colds." He nodded. There was a pause of silence. "Sorry I didn't reply to your text."

"That's okay, you've had a few busy days." She looked down at the teacup in her hands, feeling a bit awkward.

"That wasn't the reason I didn't reply. I fell asleep on the drive back, and then I thought I would see you at church, so I was just waiting to say thanks in person." Now Phoebe could see Jasper's cheeks turning a light shade of pink.

"Oh," was all Phoebe could manage. The two of them were quiet for a while and just listened the conversation that was moving around them. "Why didn't you stay with the team?" She didn't want to pry but she was curious.

"The team wanted to celebrate and go out after the game. I am not into partying. Tommy asked if we could leave early with his aunt. Thankfully, the coaches let us because sitting in a bus for three hours with a bunch of hung-over baseball guys is not enjoyable." Jasper smirked.

"I guess not." Phoebe had never been around anyone who was drunk before. Not only because she didn't really feel like she would fit in, but because it kind of scared her that alcohol could change people so much. She had heard stories from both Anna and Mary, almost always someone had done something they regretted. This was another reason people like Brittney teased her for being naïve, inexperienced, or sometimes she was called out for being an overprotected baby. She never went out to the parties on the weekends.

"So, your prom is next weekend. Any changes?" Jasper asked. At that exact moment with great force, Tabby had jumped onto the couch in-between Jasper and Tommy with her arms wrapped around their necks.

"Congratulations, you two buffoons!" she screamed.

"Tabitha!" Mrs. Anderson scolded. Tommy was laughing his head off and even Jasper was letting out a deep surprised laugh.

"She figured us out, J. Buffoon is defiantly one of our most common nicknames." Everyone laughed, and Mrs. Anderson sighed in relief to the reaction of her youngest's antics.

"Alright everyone, why don't we come to the table and enjoy this meal together?" called Mr. Anderson from the head of the table. They all squeezed in around the wooden table, as Mr. Anderson gave thanks for the food before them.

Phoebe and Jasper didn't have time to talk one on one again, as the Anderson's decided on play charades after dinner. This was helpful for Phoebe and her voice. All of them made complete fools of themselves and had each other laughing the whole time. Finally, Mrs. Anderson had to call it quits at 8:30 because Tabby had to go to bed for school in the morning. Jasper and Tommy stood to leave saying they had to get back to campus and unpack before Monday. Phoebe wondered if they were just trying to help because Tabby started to complain and cry when she was told it was bedtime. Andrew followed them out as well giving Mary a quick kiss as he went. Phoebe decided to head to bed as well in hopes to kick her sore throat. On the way to her room, she wondered what it would be like to have Jasper kiss her goodnight. She hoped one day she would get to find out.

Monday at school was the same as the week before, but even more in overdrive. Phoebe's voice had basically completely disappeared, but the scratchy pain was gone. Students were all buzzing around the school in what could only be described as summer fever. The feeling of excitement was contagious. As Phoebe went to grab her bag at the end of the day from her locker, she could see Brittney, Laura, Charlotte and to her surprise Maggie gathered in front of Brittney's locker.

"Don't we just look amazing together?" Brittney asked the girls. When Phoebe approached, she could see that Brittney had hung up the picture of her and Jasper from the news article in her locker and was now gushing over it. Phoebe opened her locker, avoiding eye contact.

"Hey, Pheebs," Maggie called. Phoebe waved to her best friend.

"Cat got your tongue Pheebs?" Brittney snickered.

"Her voice is gone," Maggie explained, thankfully, so Phoebe didn't have to try and whisper an explanation.

"Oh my gosh, you're sick? Well don't come near me. I don't want to catch whatever bug you're carrying. Prom is Saturday and I definitely don't want to be sick for that. Make sure you look for me though, if you go. I think you know my date." Brittney slammed her locker door laughing. "Are you coming, Mags? We have to go finish the rest of the homecoming court prep?"

"Sure, I'll be there in a second." Maggie walked over to lean beside Phoebe's locker. Phoebe wished she was as confident and bold as Maggie was. She was obviously defying the wishes of queen bee Brittney.

"Whatever, come on girls." Brittney sashayed down the hall with Laura and Charlotte in tow.

"How are you feeling?" Maggie asked, focusing all her attention on her.

"A lot better," Phoebe whispered smiling at her loyal BFF.

"Good. So, listen. I don't know if it is true and I don't know the details, but Britt is claiming that Jasper is taking her to prom." Phoebe stopped putting her books in her bag and starred at Maggie. "Like I said, I don't know if it is true, but I just didn't want to you to be blindsided, if they show up together on Saturday. Did he mention anything to you yesterday?" Phoebe just shook her head. She remembered him knowing that prom was this weekend, but then Tabby ambushed the conversation. Maybe, he was about to tell her that he was going with Brittney.

"Hey, Mags, you coming? Everyone is waiting?" Oliver, Maggie's new crush and prom date, called from down the hall. Maggie waved to him.

"I better get going. Maybe, you could just ask him?" *Could she just ask him?* They were at the point in their relationship where she considered him a close friend, but she felt like they were breaking through that and possibly becoming more than friends. She knew she wasn't wrong that signs were there because even her mom picked up on them. It wasn't the kind of question she wanted to ask over text. Last night while everyone was over, they filled Phoebe in that Wednesday night was the last High School and College and Careers get together before Phoebe's grade would officially switch over. Jasper, Tommy, Anna, Mary, and Andrew had all planned on going and Phoebe agreed that she wanted to go too, since she had missed out on the last one. She decided that she would confront Jasper about going to prom with Brittney there. If it was true, she knew that she would have to put him in the friend's zone, officially. Not only would going to prom alone be difficult but seeing her crush with her nemesis would be like a dagger to the heart.

Chapter Eighteen

Wednesday night had seemed to finally arrive at a snail's pace. While everyone else seemed to be counting down the days until prom on Saturday, Phoebe had been counting down the days until now. Yet, it somehow sneaked up on her and she still hadn't figured out how she wanted to ask Jasper about Brittney. Andrew had been held up at work, so he was running late to pick up the girls. Both Phoebe and Anna had suggested that they just drive themselves and meet him at HSCC, but Mary stood her ground saying that he would be arriving any minute. By the time they arrived at the church, they were twenty minutes late and everyone was listening to the college and careers pastor speaking at the front of the gym. This night must have been planned for a while because Phoebe caught on quickly that it was about abstinence and saving yourself for marriage. Phoebe didn't have a problem with the message, she fully intended on waiting, but she could see some of the other attendees shifting uncomfortably in their seats.

"I know prom is coming up for a lot of you," he said, "this can make you feel a lot of pressures to be intimate with your dates. I promise you though if you wait you won't regret it on your wedding day. Being able to give such a gift to your spouse is the best feeling for the both of you. God intended sex for man and wife. Phoebe heard some of the high school boys whispering and giggling, but she tried hard to ignore them. "If you have already given your virginity to someone else that doesn't mean you can recommit to being abstinent. Alright, I can tell by all your faces that I have talked about this enough, so let's close in prayer and enjoy the rest of our time together." As Pastor Davis prayed, Phoebe looked around the room for Jasper. Since they were so late, they had to grab the seats at the very back of the room and Mary and Andrew ended up standing against the wall. She finally spotted him with his head bowed wearing his Fendry Firehawks hat. His shoulders hunched forward, and she could tell he was focused on the prayer that she should be paying attention to as well. On one side of him was Tommy in his matching baseball hat and on the other side was Brittney who kept casting annoyed glances at him. Before Phoebe realized it, Pastor Davis had said "Amen", and everyone was on the move. They were hosting another social event so there were tables set around the room, two long tables of snacks lined against the wall. Everyone was picking up their chairs and placing them around the tables.

"Hey, Pheebs." The hair on Phoebe's neck stood on end as she turned to face the last person she thought would be at her church, Cole.

"Hi, Cole." Phoebe tried hide to both her shock and her cringe, but she felt that Cole could see right through her.

"I thought I saw you come in. My cousin Angela goes here, and our parents thought it would be a good idea if I came with her. At first, I was dreading it but that was before I knew you would be here." His toothy grin slide across his face making her feel even more uncomfortable. She looked around the room hoping one of her sisters or Andrew would see her call for help.

"That's cool. I hope you enjoy the night," she said, trying to signal the end of the conversation.

"Oh, I am sure I will." Cole took a small step towards her looking Phoebe up and down. How did she think he was such a nice guy before? "Why don't we go get some food together. It would be nice to chat about other things than the bakery." Cole put his hand on the middle of Phoebe's back making her jump a little.

"Hey, Phoebe," a deep voice broke into the awkward and uncomfortable situation. "Tommy and I saved you a spot. Are you coming?" Phoebe looked up at Jasper's handsome scruff covered face. He wasn't looking at her but was holding his gaze on Cole. Cole immediately dropped his hand from her back.

"Thanks, I was just about to come over," Phoebe said as calmly as she could. "It was nice to see you Cole, have a good night."

"Yeah, you too," he sputtered and walked away to his cousin Angela who was grabbing a plate of snacks.

"Thanks for coming to save me." Phoebe turned to Jasper.

"No problem, you looked a little uncomfortable."

"Yeah, the more I get to know Cole, the more unsettled I feel," she told him.

"You're not the first person I have heard that from. Why don't you go sit down and I'll grab us some snacks and a drink." Jaspers gestured to the snack table where Cole was now talking to Brittney and some other girls.

"That would be great." Phoebe walked calmly over to the table Tommy, Anna and some of Anna's friends were sitting at. Phoebe liked Anna's friends. She hadn't met them much because they also lived on campus. They were a part of the cheer squad and they had been to her house a couple times. Devon Chen sat next to Anna leaning her chin on her hands, engulfed in the conversation. She, of course, was just as stunning as Anna, but in different ways. Her mother was from Jamaica and her father was from Japan, she told them the story of how they met in Australia on a mission's trip. Her long black hair was in thick dreads down to her waist. Today, she had put on thick black eyeliner that accentuated her cat-like eyes even more. Phoebe loved Devon's loud and energetic personality; she always had some sort of funny quip or saying to add to a conversation. Samantha Jean was Anna's other best friends and the opposite personality wise from Devon. She was quiet and reserved, always seeming to be relaxed like she had just finished one of her yoga classes she taught. She had dark brown long hair that always appeared to be in the perfect wave. Her eyes were as blue as Anna's. She always reminded Phoebe of a Disney princess. She was leaning back on her chair, sipping her green tea. She was also very health conscious, being vegan and only choosing to eat organic. Of course, all three girls sitting at the table were laughing at a story Tommy was telling. Phoebe took the seat on the other side of Samantha. She smiled at her as Tommy continued to tell a story about how the coach on one of the opposing teams they faced this year always had chocolate smeared on his pants. Apparently, he ate chocolate when he was stressed and the heat from his hands would melt it, which he would then rub off on the seat of his pants. The poor guy didn't realize that it looked like he was having bathroom troubles.

"Remember Coach Patrick?" Tommy asked, laughing as soon as Jasper appeared at the table. His lopsided grin appeared on his scruffy face. Even though his hat disguised his eyes, Phoebe could tell there was a twinkle of humor in them.

"Yeah, poor guy. People started calling him Coach P for a whole other reason." Tommy bent forward in a fit of laughter and Devon almost spit out her water. These two were going to be a fun filled combination. There were three empty seats between Tommy and Phoebe at their round table of eight. Jasper placed a plate down in front of Phoebe and two water bottles. "I figured we could just share a plate. Is that okay?" He asked sitting down beside her. Her heart swooned over the intimacy of sharing a plate way more than a normal person should. She was also ecstatic that he chose to sit beside her instead of his best friend.

"That's fine. Thanks for getting the snacks and water." Anna caught her eye as Jasper grabbed a cookie off their shared plate. Just by her facial expression, she could tell Anna was freaking out too.

The rest of the night carried on with great conversation at their table. Often, other groups would look over because they would be laughing or talking so loudly. Phoebe was right that Tommy and Devon took charge of the conversation for the most part, but Phoebe did not mind one bit. A couple of times, some other people would stop by briefly to say hi or join the conversation. Anna would always make sure to introduce Phoebe if it was someone she hadn't met from the College and Careers group. Phoebe was having so much fun she couldn't believe it when Pastor Davis called for everyone's attention, thanking all of them for coming and closing the night off with prayer. Andrew and Mary walked over to their table hand in hand.

"Hate to break up the party over here but are you ladies ready to go?" Andrew greeted them. Phoebe realized that she never got the chance to ask Jasper about Brittney. She decided not to bring it up anymore. If they were really a thing, wouldn't he have been sitting with her all night instead of Phoebe?

"Yes, we are. I don't think my stomach can handle anymore cookies or laughing." Anna stood up and gave quick hugs around the necks to both of her best friends. "Thanks for a wonderful evening, everyone." She beamed at them all. Phoebe wished she was that graceful. Instead, she stood up and gave a small wave to everyone.

"We should actually be heading back too." Devon stood up after her quick hug with Anna. "I know I will probably crash soon, and we have early cheer tomorrow."

"I totally forgot about cheer! I should have brought some stuff with me and stayed over with you guys," Anna whined.

"We can take you back to campus with us if you think your parents would be okay with it," Tommy suggested to Anna.

"I appreciate the offer, but I am not sure if that would go over well with my parents; plus, I am not ready at all." Anna was right, even though the Andersons knew Tommy and Jasper, letting Anna go to campus with them alone at night was not something they would let any of their girls do. They still weren't totally comfortable with Mary going around with Andrew all the time, but now that she was and "adult" they realized they didn't have much say.

"No problem," Tommy reassured. It was nice because they knew he was being genuine and would not be offended. Phoebe knew that Anna had struggled a lot with her friends complaining how strict their parents were. She could see on Anna's face that she appreciated the understanding. It was hard when friends complained, teased, or bashed their parents. They all walked out to the parking lot together. By coincidence, Andrew had parked right beside Jasper's truck.

"Are you excited for prom on Saturday?" Jasper asked again quietly as he walked beside Phoebe.

"I guess so," She shrugged. She thought about asking him about Brittney came into mind, but she knew for sure after tonight that her feelings for Jasper were not going to change either way. She might have more heartache if he was going with Brittney, but it wouldn't prevent her from being interested in him.

"That doesn't sound very positive," Jasper laughed bumping his hip against hers.

"Nothing has changed from the last time we talked. I am still flying solo, which is fine," she added quickly, "but I still would have rather gone with my friends. It will be fun to see everyone all dressed up though." She smiled up at him.

"You never know what could happen. I never went to my prom, remember? Just enjoy the experience as much as you can. I kind of feel like I missed that rite of passage, as silly as that sounds," Jasper shrugged as they came to a stop in front of their vehicles.

"Thanks again for the entertainment tonight!" Tommy laughed as he got into Jasper's truck.

"See you around." Jasper smiled at Phoebe, hopping in his vehicle. Off they went leaving Phoebe smiling as she watched.

Chapter Nineteen

The next morning, Phoebe hustled into the school determined to focus on finishing all her independent studies and assignments so that she didn't have to worry about them. She also wanted them to be off her plate so she could have fun at prom and then look forward to her graduation that would follow soon after. Graduation! She couldn't even believe how fast the past four years went; now she was going to go to Fendry. Soon, she could officially call herself a Firehawk. She envisioned herself walking to classes in a red sweater sporting the famous bird and then after cheering Jasper and Tommy on at their games. With college also came more freedom; Phoebe was excited for all the possibilities.

"Honestly, I don't know what all the hype about him is. The more time I spent with him, the more time I realized how boring he was. I mean he didn't even stay to celebrate with his teammates on their last win of the season. He doesn't even drink. Talk about dud. Talk about selfish." Phoebe's ear tweaked as she approached her locker near Brittney who was obviously bashing Jasper to one of her best friends, Charlotte.

"Totally," Charlotte said, nodding her head along to Brittney's venting session. So, the tension Phoebe had felt between Jasper and Brittney wasn't wrong.

"I am so glad I met Cole. Did I tell you about how funny he was? He was making me laugh all night. We are going to hang out after school today. He is going to come pick me up." Brittney slammed her locker door and turned quickly without even an ounce of attention towards Phoebe. Her long blonde hair swishing behind her.

"So, I take it you know that Jasper and Brittney aren't a thing," Maggie laughed coming up behind scaring Phoebe. Maggie laughed at Phoebe's shocked reaction.

"I guess not. They didn't talk at all yesterday at HCSS; but she must have had a good time with Cole." Phoebe grabbed her books for homeroom.

"Must've, because she said to switch her prom court date name to his in our group messages late last night. Then went on about how she dumped Jasper." Phoebe's eyes widen in shock. "Don't worry. We all know it isn't true. Even Oliver said the guys were so sick of her."

"Do you think I should warn her about Cole?" Phoebe asked.

"Are you kidding? First, that woman is a tornado, and you should be warning Cole about her, and second, no way will whatever is going on between them last." Maggie flicked her hand as if she was brushing dust under the rug. "I just wanted to remind you that I will be at your place around two on Saturday to get ready! You are sure that Anna is okay with helping us? I feel bad."

"She is more than okay. She had already made a schedule of manicure, pedicures, makeup, and hair for us. I think she is more excited than we are," Phoebe chuckled. "Two o'clock is perfect. Can you text Jenn to remind her?"

"I already did." Of course, she had, Maggie would run the world one day and make it look easy. Phoebe never knew how she could keep up with all her volunteering, extra curriculars, schoolwork, etc. She was amazing. "I probably won't get to see you or talk much until then with all the loose ends that need tying. So, I will see you Saturday!" Maggie gave her a quick hug and walked away. She picked up her pace and heading to her homeroom down the hall from Phoebe's, not wanting to be late.

Maggie was right. Phoebe hadn't seen or heard from her the rest of the week. She ate lunch with Jenn and her now boyfriend Josh. Phoebe couldn't believe that Jenn was dating someone. Apparently, even her dad liked him. She was over the moon for her friend who was clearly smitten. Lunch on Friday, Phoebe ate in the biology classroom to finish up her last project, which she very happily handed in on the teacher's desk. The last thing she had to complete was her English essay and she was officially done until exams, which all her teachers promised would be light in leu of all the projects they had assigned. She definitely wasn't going to complain about that. The last bell on Friday was like sweet music to her ears. She could not wait to get home. She texted with Jasper briefly on Thursday, but hadn't heard from him since that morning. Tommy had also messaged her asking what the special at the Bakery was tomorrow. He literally was always thinking about food. It made her laugh. Her plan was to go home, organize her work things for tomorrow morning, and get all the items she needed for prom ready. She promised Anna she would help set up a get ready station in the living room. Her parents agreed the living room would be the best spot. After that, all she wanted to do was text Jasper and watch a movie.

Her hopes of an easy Friday night were crashed by her family. Her mom asked her to help Tabby pack for a birthday party sleepover that she was going to and drop her off. Helping Tabby do anything was always an event. Her stubborn independence always took over. She had to do everything herself and would not take advice from Phoebe. Phoebe finally stopped fighting Tabby and shoved in some sensible pjs, water bottle, and her stuffed animal when she wasn't looking. Phoebe knew she would not be able to sleep without it, no matter how embarrassed she was of it. She finally dropped Tabby off at the party thirty minutes late and breathed a breath of relief. She did not know how her mom handled her strong willed youngest every day. Phoebe was backing out of the driveway when her mom called. Connecting to Bluetooth, she answered the phone.

"Hey, mom; I just dropped Tabby off."

"Thanks, Pheebs, I really appreciate it. Would you mind doing me another favour?" her mom asked.

"Sure," Phoebe tried not to feel annoyed. She knew her mom wouldn't ask unless she really needed help, but all she wanted to do was sit on the couch and chill out.

"Mary was supposed to pick up the pizza for dinner tonight but now she is doing a group assignment late at school. She was also supposed to pick up Anna from cheer. Could you do that?" her mom was huffing and puffing.

"No problem. Mom, are you okay? You sound winded." Phoebe turned the opposite direction from home and headed to grab Anna from Fendry.

"Oh, fine. I am just trying to get the house sorted for tomorrow's fun. Vacuuming the stairs is always a workout."

"Mom, I could have done that!" Phoebe exclaimed. "It's just Maggie and Jenn coming tomorrow. They have been at our house so many times, you do not have to super clean for them."

"I know, but it's a special day tomorrow and I want you girls to have an amazing time and have great memories. I had a wonderful time at my Prom. I just want the same for you." Phoebe smiled. She loved her mom and hoped that she could serve her own family one day like her mom served them. She always put her kids and husband first.

"Thanks, Mom, you're the best."

"Thanks for getting your sister and don't forget the pizza. It's at Eddie's Pizza under Anderson. I have already paid for it, so you just need to pick it up." Eddie's Pizza was their family's usual pizza shop. Her dad wouldn't eat any other pizza; well, besides her mom's homemade.

"See you in a bit." Phoebe pressed end on the screen and let the music on the radio fill the air. She, for sure, was not going to get to relax tonight now. Not with her mom cleaning like crazy and she still had to help Anna set up. She decided to use the next twenty minutes as her own. She opened the window and drummed along to the song playing on the radio.

Anna was already sitting in the parking lot talking to a group of cheerleaders and football players. Phoebe had to laugh about how stereotypical the image was. All the guys were in their football pads with their helmets off while the cheerleaders wore their red and black practice uniforms, pom-poms held on their hips. She gave a light honk of the horn, notifying Anna of her arrival. Anna smiled and waved to everyone. Phoebe heard a couple of the guys call after her waving, clearly trying to capture the last seconds of her attention. Anna gave them a sweet smile and jumped into the passenger seat of the car.

"Hey, Pheebs, thanks for coming to get me!" Her voice came out in a high pitch over-the-top happy sound.

"Hey, can you leave the cheer voice outside," Phoebe exaggerated her cringe. Anna laughed and waved out the window to her group of friends as they drove away.

"Sorry, cheer was great today and then the football team came over to tell us how much they appreciated us. I am just in a really good mood. Oh, and of course, I am so excited for tomorrow to get you ladies already for the prom." Anna clapped her hands together like she was still doing a cheer. Phoebe had to smile at her older sister. She was infectious and Phoebe needed that.

"Are you sure those guys weren't just flirting with you?" Phoebe asked.

"Oh, it's possible, but they know I am not interested in them. We just like to banter. It's all in fun."

"Okay…" Phoebe knew those guys definitely wanted more with Anna, but her sister obviously did not want to even entertain a conversation about it.

"So, have you decided on a hair? Do you like any of the photos I showed you this week?" They talked about prom and how Phoebe wanted her to do her hair, nails, and makeup the rest of the way home and then as they ate dinner. It felt really weird to Phoebe, having all the attention on her since it was only her, Anna, and her parents home. Even her dad had made some comments here and there throughout the conversation, which was especially weird since he normally avoided all talk about makeup and hair. After they had their fill of pizza, the three Anderson women set to work making the living room into a salon. Phoebe and Anna tried to get their mom to relax, but she insisted she wanted to help and that she was having fun. They didn't finish everything until ten o'clock that night, but the living room looked amazing. They had set up a table and chairs with bowls and towels for manicures; then Phoebe's dad's reclining chair would be used for pedicures. Anna had put together a folding table that was now covered with hairspray, gels, curlers, styling wands and brushes. Mrs. Anderson had hung Phoebe's dress on the curtain rod and placed her shoes underneath it, just as you would see in a wedding day photo. They had also picked out old chick flicks that they would put on while Anna made them over. It was all making Phoebe really excited for tomorrow with her friends. The panic of having to attend prom by herself was being washed away. The more excited she got, the more confident she felt like she could arrive and have fun single.

"I think we are all set," Anna said looking triumphantly around the room.

"Thank you so much again for doing this. I know it will be a lot of work, but Maggie, Jenn and I are all so happy and thankful." Phoebe gave her sister a huge hug.

"Honestly, I think I am more excited than you. This will be a great experience for me, and I really appreciate you guys letting me take photos for my book."

"Alright, girls, I think we should all go get some rest before tomorrow. Phoebe, are you sure you're going to be okay to work tomorrow? You know Mrs. Baker said you could have it off."

"I'm sure. It will help make the day go faster. I don't think I could sit around here and wait patiently," Phoebe replied.

"Well, off to bed then. I love you both and I will see you in the morning." Mrs. Anderson made her exit downstairs to her retreat with her husband. Phoebe and Anna both took their mother's advice and headed straight to bed. As soon as Phoebe's head hit the pillow, she was fast asleep with exhaustion.

Chapter Twenty

Phoebe felt like a zombie, as she put her things away in the office at the bakery. Although she slept, it was one of those sleeps where it felt like six minutes instead of hours. She shuffled herself to the front counter and grabbed the fresh pot of coffee with an extra-large cup.

"Woah, late night last night, Pheebs?" She nearly dumped the whole pot down the front of her at the sound of Cole's voice. "So, what was it? Late night study sesh or should I be jealous of a late-night friend's visit?" Phoebe knew exactly what he was insinuating, and she didn't like it.

"Neither of those, Cole," she responded as she pushed by him to the kitchen.

"So, why do you need all the caffeine? Were you up late last night thinking about me?" He gave her a slimy wink.

"Only in my nightmares." Phoebe couldn't believe that she let that slip from her mouth. It was so unkind. If her mother had heard her, she would have been reprimanded immediately. However, it didn't seem to deter Cole, but rather made him laugh.

"I have never seen this side of you, Pheebs. I think I like it." Each time he said her nickname, he stressed the E making her stomach turn.

"Cole, can you, please, fill up the ingredients in the kitchen and stock the front counter?" Thankfully, Mrs. Barker had hustled in at the perfect time, saving Phoebe from anymore of Cole's quips. Cole gave Phoebe another wink and flexed his arms before picking up a big bag of flour.

"That boy," Mrs. Barker shook her head. "If he bothers you, make sure you let me know, but I think he is just looking for attention. The fact that he isn't getting it from you is making him crazy. I think he likes the chase." Phoebe waved it off and continued to sip her coffee. As much as Cole gave her the creeps, she didn't think it would escalate any farther than his annoying comments.

Mrs. Barker and Phoebe set to work making cinnamon buns, pecan tarts, scones, and chocolate chip cookies to fill up the empty spots in the display case. Phoebe loved working with Mrs. Barker; she always had the best stories and her life seemed like it was full adventure. By the time Phoebe's shift had come to an end, she was in a much better mood and felt energized and excited to get home for her prom get ready party.

"Thank you so much for coming in, Phoebe." Mrs. Barker smiled and continued to mix the batter for a special-order black forest cake. "I hope you have marvelous time at your prom, dear, and, please, take a picture of yourself with your friends! I want to live vicariously through you. Remember to make smart choices, ones that you won't be disappointed with in the future. Next time, I'll have to tell you about my prom. I went with a real looker named Tommy." Mrs. Barker's gaze drifted away like she was reminiscing. Then she gave a quick wave. "Next time! Have fun." Phoebe laughed.

"See you next week." She was grabbing her bag from the office when Cole appeared in the doorway startling her. "Gosh, Cole, do you have to scare me all the time?"

"Sorry, maybe I should start wearing a bell. Then you'll know where I am at all times." His grin spread from ear to ear. Phoebe ignored him putting her bag over her shoulder and grabbing the box of cinnamon buns Mrs. Barker told her to bring home for her family and friends. "I just wanted to say I'll see you later tonight... at prom."

"What?" Then Phoebe remember that Maggie told her Brittney was taking Cole as her date.

"I'm going with Britt. I guess she told Jasper to take a hike and thought I would be a better choice. I must admit, I agree." Cole paused as if to wait for Phoebe to say she agreed as well. She didn't. "Just because I am going with Britt, doesn't mean I can't save a dance for you. You don't think your date would mind, would they?" Phoebe had never wished more in her life than this moment that she did have a date. She wanted to say so badly that her date would mind so she would not be able to dance with him. Instead, she said:

"I think all your dances will be taken by your date, but thanks for the offer." She moved to the backdoor, praying that she got away with that response, but no such luck.

"So, no date, then?" Cole leaned against the doorframe of the office, starring at her.

"I am going with my friends." Before he could respond with any further comments or questions, she pushed open the backdoor and sped walked to her car. She let out a huge sigh of relief as she started the engine. Shaking her shoulders and putting her car in reverse she told herself to get in the mind-set of fun. This would be a core memory, and she wanted it to be a great one.

When Phoebe got home, Tabby came running to her. Her mom must have picked her up from the sleep over earlier this morning.

"You got a huge bouquet of flowers!" Tabby squealed running back into the kitchen.

"What?" Phoebe asked in shocked. She walked into the kitchen putting down the box of cinnamon buns to find a beautiful bouquet of white and light pink flowers. It was stunning. A card was placed on stick in the middle of it. "Who are they from?" Phoebe asked Tabby, who was sitting on top of the counter beside them.

"I don't know! Mom said I couldn't open the card. I tried to a bunch of times, but she always caught me before I could." Phoebe laughed. "Can you, please, open the card I am dying to know. It is eating me alive." Phoebe rolled her eyes at her little sister dramatics, but to be honest it felt like it was eating her alive as well. She lifted the little white card from the delicate flowers. The envelope only read "Phoebe". Opening it up she pulled out a yellow piece of card stock that read: *Phoebe - Happy Prom. You deserve to have a night to remember.* That was it. Phoebe flipped over the card to see if it was signed on the back, but there was nothing to say who it was from.

"Come on! I waited all that time for that! Who is it from? I'm calling the flower company." Tabby jumped off the counter and ran off to find the phone.

"I see you found your flowers," her mom said, walking into the kitchen.

"I did. Are they from you and dad?" That would make sense. It was something her dad would do. He always bought all four of his daughters flowers on Valentine's Day.

"No, they aren't. I must admit I wanted to open the card too. I almost let Tabby." Her mom laughed.

"The flower company said if there was no name on the card then they can't release the information of who purchased them." Tabby flung herself into the dining room chair next to the kitchen and put her chin on her hands in frustration. "What a bust! Oh, I know, I should call them back and say we are afraid your stalker is back and we need to know right away who they are from for your safety!"

"Tabitha, where do you get these ideas from? Don't even think about it." Phoebe's mom wagged her finger at her with a stern glare. "Well, I guess it is a mystery. Maybe, it will solve itself later." Mrs. Anderson shrugged with a twinkle in her eye. Phoebe wondered if she knew something about it and wasn't saying anything. "You should go have a shower, Phoebe, and blow-dry your hair. Anna gave me strict instructions to tell you that. She ran out to the store in the van to get a nail polish that matched your dress."

"Okay." Phoebe was still in shock about the flowers and the mystery sender. Who could they be from? She secretly hoped they were from Jasper, but she still hadn't heard anything from him since Thursday. She had sent him a couple 'Hey, how are you?' messages, but after two with no reply she decided not to send anymore.

"Earth to Phoebe? Your friends are going to be here in an hour, so you should get moving." Phoebe turned to look at her mom, who had found the cinnamon buns and were placing them on a serving platter. Hopefully, the mystery would be solved soon just like her mom said.

By the time Phoebe had finished her shower, blow-dried her long brown hair and applied her moisturizer she heard laughing and music playing downstairs. The smell of baked goods and coffee floated up into her room. She smiled to herself in excitement for an afternoon of pampering with her friends. Maggie and Jenn were both already sitting at the dining room table with

Phoebe's mom having coffee. Her mom had hung their dresses up next to Phoebe's on the curtain rod. The dresses were all completely different, but each one was beautiful.

"Jenn, I can't believe you made that dress!" Phoebe exclaimed running over to look at the stunning dress her best friend had been working on for months. It was a shimmering white material, which Jenn had painstakingly embroidered vibrant flowers all over. It looked like it was more fitted on the top and would float out towards the bottom. Phoebe carefully touched the delicate cup sleeves.

"Thanks," Jenn beamed from her seat. "I am really happy with it. Mrs. Vani said that she loved it as well and was expecting to see my name in big lights on a runway one day." Phoebe could tell Jenn was over the moon about that high praise. Mrs. Vani was a hard one to please and was very knowledgeable when it came to fashion. Not wanting to forget the beauty of Maggie's dress Phoebe gawked over it as well. It was a bright fitted magenta colour with a square neck like and thin straps. The whole thing was covered in sparkles. Maggie talked about how she had a hard time deciding on a dress, but felt that this one really made her features popped. She was also able to order a matching tie and pocket square for Oliver that he had promised to wear. The girls continued to talk fast with excitement about their dresses and shoes. Mrs. Anderson smiled as she placed fruit, baked goods, candy and more at the dining room table. Mary and Andrew had taken Tabby out to play mini putt and then were going to take her to dinner so that the girls could enjoy their time together without Tabby bouncing around. Phoebe was thankful for that. She loved her little sister, but she could be a handful sometimes. All of her family members had come together to really make this a special day for her. She felt loved.

"Hello, ladies!" Anna bounded through the door with Devon and another girl Phoebe hadn't met before. "I hope you are all are ready for an afternoon of pampering!" Anna clapped her hands together and Jenn let out a hoot. "These are my friends, Devon and Angela. They have come to help me. When I told them what I was doing today, they thought each of you should have the focus of a dedicated stylist." Phoebe was in shock. She thought it was just going to be Anna doing everything. Devon and Angela joined the dining room table and Phoebe walked over to Anna who was putting out the new nail polishes she got from the store.

"Um, are you sure your friends want to be doing this? If it was too much, I wish you would have said something to me." Phoebe bit her lip feeling awkward.

"Not at all, Pheebs, they actually really want to help and when they found out they could use pictures of you guys for their book they were excited. Are you not okay with it? I am sorry I should have asked you. I wanted it to be a surprise."

"No, it's fine." Phoebe shook her head. "I just feel bad."

"Don't! Enjoy this, Pheebs. This is what we want to do for a living and all the practice; it's helpful. Think of it as doing us a favour." Anna gave Phoebe a squeeze on the shoulders. "And don't worry. I am going to be your stylist today. I couldn't let anyone else get my little sister ready for prom." Her sister had done all this for her, her mom was serving them like queens and Mary was helping by taking Tabby out. Everyone was coming together to make sure she had a great time. She felt so special. "Alright, ladies let's get this party started." Anna turned up the music and started dancing. Devon grabbed Maggie's hand and Angela grabbed Jenn's, they all started moving their hips to the beat and giggling. Even Phoebe's mom was clapping her hands and then waving them in the air. Phoebe knew this would be a day she would always remember.

Chapter Twenty-One

Mrs. Anderson brought up her full-length mirror, so the girls could see themselves. Phoebe knew her friends were beautiful before, but now with their makeup and nails done and wearing stunning dresses they looked like they could walk the red carpet. Maggie had chosen to do a simple light pink on both her toenails and fingers. She felt like her dress was bold enough. She somehow managed to find matching magenta shoes. Her hair was pulled back into a long shiny ponytail. Not a strand was out of place. Her makeup accentuated her cheeks and her eyes. Jenn went with a bright blue on her toenails that peaked out from her white stilettos. She chose a bright pink for her fingernails. Both nail polishes matched one of the colours that she used to embroider the flowers on her dress. Her makeup was the most dramatic of the girls. She went with a bold blue cat wing eye and sparkles on her cheeks. Her hair was pulled back into a low bun that Anna had called a chignon. Everything about the way Jenn looked displayed her personality. Phoebe was in awe of her friends. She had yet to look at herself in the mirror. Anna wanted to capture it on camera. She ended up choosing to wear the dark green nail polish Anna had found to match her dress on her toes, and a soft light pink on her fingernails. Anna had drawn a cute little heart on each ring fingernail in white. Phoebe loved it. She decided to wear her hair long and down, but Anna had styled it with waterfall waves that made it look like she was from the 1950s. Phoebe had told Anna that she wanted a more natural looking makeup, but wanted her eyes to pop. Anna had even applied fake eyelashes, which Phoebe was still getting use to. She felt like she had to blink a million times, when they were first put on. She took a deep breath, before looking in the mirror.

"Is that really me!?" She gasped at her reflection. She knew it was her, but she looked pretty. He blue eyes looked like the ocean and were accentuated by the lashes. She had a glow on her cheeks that made her look fresh and alive. She had never felt this way before. She wasn't just plain old Phoebe anymore. Everyone giggled at her reactions, and it was met with a bunch of "of course, that's you", "you look amazing", and "you're a model". Phoebe was still trying to take it all in, when her dad snuck up behind her and gave her a hug.

"My little girl isn't so little anymore. I hope you know that you are beautiful, even in your sweats or jeans. Your heart is the most beautiful part of you, Phoebe. The outside of you is matching it tonight." Phoebe held back her tears. Her dad never said such tender things to her before. She felt like she was glowing. "Just make sure you are yourself always. Don't change for anyone. You are an amazing woman of God, Phoebe Anderson. I am so honoured and thankful He gave you to me." Phoebe nodded her head to show her dad that she was listening. She knew if she tried to speak, she would cry and mess up the awesome makeup job Anna had done.

"Alright, girls, let's get some pictures taken before your dates come to pick you up. I promised your parents lots of them. Also, you ladies cannot leave until I take some with your dates. Maggie, your mom gave me a list." Mrs. Anderson shooed the girls outside in the backyard to take the photos by a trellis that was growing beautiful white flowers. They all took individual photos, photos in pairs, photos all together and photos with their personal stylists. Phoebe was taking a few pictures with her parents when Anna came out and announced that Josh was here to pick up Jenn. Jenn let out a squeal and smoothed out her hair and dress. Phoebe was having so much fun that she forgot she wasn't going to go to the prom with her friends. They had dates and she didn't. The wind felt like it was taken out of Phoebe's sails a bit, but she tried to disguise her sadness with a smile plastered on her face. She held her shoulders back, reminding herself of all wonderful things her mom said about her the other day and the things her father had just whispered. She was a confident woman of God. She could do this. It would just be another step in her journey of finding Phoebe.

"You look perfect, Jenn," Phoebe said, giving her friend's hand a squeeze. Josh walked outside in a bright blue suit that match the blue on Jenn's dress.

He had a white shirt on with no tie, leaving a few buttons on the top undone. Phoebe thought he looked very rocker handsome. He matched Jenn well.

"Wow, you look fantastic!" He exclaimed coming over and kissing Jenn on the cheek. He held out a colourful corsage of carnations that matched the boutonniere he had. They looked at each other smiling. Phoebe couldn't help but feel jealous. What a special moment this was for them. Even if they didn't end up together forever, they would remember his moment, just as Mrs. Barker remembered hers all those year ago.

Mrs. Anderson set Josh and Jenn up under the trellis and started taking photos of them, while everyone watched and encouraged them to do cute poses.

"Hey, everyone," came a voice from the deck off the kitchen. All of them turned to find Oliver standing at the screen door. He had on a dark blue suit with his magenta tie and pocket square shining proudly on his chest. Phoebe already knew that Oliver was good looking. He was one of the most popular guys in school, being a part of the L.I.O.Ns, but those qualities really shined through as he walked down to meet Maggie on the grass. He had on a simple white orchid boutonniere, which matched the wrist corsage he was now placing on Maggie's arm.

"Thank you, it's so beautiful," Maggie said, smiling up at her date.

"Not as beautiful as you," Phoebe heard Oliver reply. She felt awkward like she was an intruder on their private moment. She slowly backed away, feeling a haze of doubt and insecurity flood over her again.

"Maggie and Oliver, it's your turn to take some photos. I have the list your mom wanted here on my phone. Let's get started. There are quite a few and I don't want you to be late!" Mrs. Anderson started ushering them under the trellis.

"Well, I think we will get going now that our pictures are done," Josh announced. "Phoebe, you look great." He nodded and smiled at her.

"Thanks, you too." She gave a little wave to Jenn as she passed by clinging to Josh's arm chattering away about their afternoon of pamper. Phoebe stood next to Anna continuing to watch as Maggie and Oliver fulfilled the list of poses Maggie's mom wanted.

"How are you doing, Pheebs?" Anna asked her. She could see a little pity in Anna's eyes.

"I am okay. I was having such a fun time this afternoon. I forgot all about this part." She shrugged. "Thanks again for all the work you did. It was so fun, and you made me feel really special and beautiful."

"That's because you are Phoebe. Don't forget that." Anna gave her a squeeze and then fixed a stray hair on her forehead. "Just because you aren't going with a date, doesn't mean that you won't have a great time." Phoebe knew Anna was right, but she just really didn't want to have to walk in there all alone. The thought of finding a table and then sitting by herself during the slow dances started making her feel queasy. She smoothed down the front of her dress, trying to push the horrible stomach feeling away.

"Thank you again for everything today. It was so much fun!" Maggie said, addressing the styling team and Phoebe's parents. "We should get going." She beamed up at Oliver who was the image of perfection. Even his smile was perfectly straight and white. They looked like a political couple you would see in a newspaper.

"Our pleasure. Have a great night you two. Be safe!" Mrs. Anderson called. Maggie stepped closely to Phoebe, on her way back into the house.

"Do you want to ride with us, Pheebs?" she asked in a quiet voice.

"Oh, no, I am fine. This is a date for you guys. I refuse to be the third wheel," Phoebe said plastering a fake smile on once again.

"Are you sure? I asked Oliver and he doesn't mind at all." Oliver was now waiting at the sliding doors talking to Phoebe's dad. She thought about taking Maggie up on her offer for a minute but knew that she shouldn't.

"No, I am honestly okay, but thank you for the offer," She reassured Maggie.

"Okay. See you there soon. I will save you a spot at our table." Maggie gave her a little wave and walked to her date, leaving Phoebe behind.

"Are you sure you don't want to go with them, sweetie? I really don't think they would mind," Mrs. Anderson questioned. Phoebe felt a little embarrassed that her mom overhead their conversation. She was feeling so many emotions and was trying to hold it together.

"I am sure. I can do this you guys. I don't need anyone to go to prom with me. I am a strong independent woman of God." Phoebe puffed out her chest and laughed trying to not only diffuse the tension but trying to convince herself of her own words.

"Yes, you are, sweetie." Her mom held her hand as they walked inside to grab Phoebe's small clutch with her keys and phone. "Remember to call us when you get there and before you leave. Your dad says you have to be home by 12:30 the absolute latest." Phoebe nodded along to the list of instructions her mom rattled off. "I know I don't have to say this, but I am doing my motherly duty, no drinking." Phoebe reassured her mom that she would not be drinking and would be home on time.

"Alright, Pheebs," Anna stepped in front of her, "here is the lipstick I used on you and a small comb that will fit in your bag. Just do light brushes, okay?" Anna gave her air kisses on each cheek. Suddenly, the doorbell rang making all of the Andersons freeze. No one moved, not even to answer the door.

"Someone must have forgotten something." Mrs. Anderson and Phoebe moved to the front door together. Phoebe's eyes grew with surprise at the sight of him. He was standing there in a black suite with a boutonniere to match the pink and white flowers that had been sent to her earlier today. In one of his hands was a matching corsage and in the other was a baseball with the words 'PROM?' written on it.

"Oh my," Mrs. Anderson let out a gasp of shock.

"Phoebe Anderson," he said, "Can I take you to prom?"

For more information contact info@advbooks.com

we bring dreams to life™
advbookstore.com